A challenge was just what the killer needed, something special.

The killer was more than just a hit man. That's all most of them were, hit men. This one, however, was an artist, and as such would accept nothing short of perfection. When that knife had sunk to the hilt in the stomach of victim number twenty-four, that had been perfection.

A challenge such as victim number twenty-five would be something very, very special.

"All right," the killer said, "who is it?"

The killer could feel the dramatic pause that the other man was using to set up the final revelation. When it finally came, however, it was worth the wait.

"Nick Carter," said the client. "The name is Nick Carter."

The killer had been right. This was perfect, but not only that, it was special—which was only fitting, since the killer was known throughout the espionage world as the Specialist.

And the Specialist vs. the Killmaster—well, that was very special indeed.

NICK CARTER IS IT!

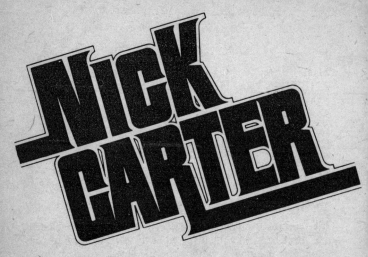

NICK CARTER

PLEASURE ISLAND

CHARTER
NEW YORK
A Division of Charter Communications Inc.
A GROSSET & DUNLAP COMPANY
51 Madison Avenue
New York, New York 10010

PLEASURE ISLAND

An Ace Charter Original.

First Ace Charter Printing October 1981
Published simultaneously in Canada
Manufactured in the United States of America

2 4 6 8 0 9 7 5 3 1

PLEASURE ISLAND

Dedicated to the Men of the
Secret Services of the
United States of America

Prologue

The twenty-fourth victim looked both ways before crossing the dark, wet London street. As far as he knew, he was meeting an informant who was to give him some information on a shipment of drugs worth millions that was coming into London on its way to the United States.

But what he was doing was rendezvousing with his own death.

It waited for him in an alley; dark, quiet, and deadly.

The twenty-fourth victim had a knife in a wrist sheath, and he was confident that he could handle anything that came his way by using that knife. Perhaps he was even overconfident, but that knife was his specialty, and when he had it with him he felt totally confident. His reputation in the world of espionage was as one of the best blade men around—if not the best.

With his left hand he touched the knife in its sheath, just to reassure himself. He entered the alley mouth, listening intently. The only sound he could hear was the noise that last night's raindrops made as they fell from the rooftops to the street below. The only other audible sound was that of his own footsteps as he entered the alley and walked deeper and deeper until he reached a dimly lit cul-de-sac.

He assumed that he was the first to arrive.

He was wrong.

He was being watched from a darkened doorway by a figure who was remaining totally still and quiet. The figure in the doorway was going to let his victim wait, hoping that he would become edgy as he waited. The figure intended to take the man out with his own weapon, a knife. For that, every advantage would help, and if the man became nervous to any extent, that would be an advantage.

The intended victim wanted a cigarette but knew enough not to light one. He'd have to do without. It was past the appointed time, and still his informant had not shown up. He was becoming annoyed, both because he wanted a cigarette and because the man was late.

Or not coming.

Five minutes later, he was just plain pissed.

It was time.

The darkened figure stepped from the doorway, purposely scraping a foot to announce the arrival of a second party.

The victim turned, eyes wide, momentarily startled.

"What the hell—" he exclaimed. "Jesus, but you're quiet. You been there the whole time?"

The figure did not answer. The other man could not make out any identifiable features. The shape in front of him seemed to be just that—a shape.

"You're quiet," he said again.

"You're dead," the shape said.

"Wha—"

Suddenly there was an identifiable item for the victim to make out. He knew it very well.

He knew what a knife, gleaming in a shaft of moonlight, looked like.

He adapted himself to the situation immediately, because he was a pro. He shook his head and flicked his wrist and his knife nestled comfortably—and comfortingly—in his palm.

"You made a mistake," he told the dark shape in front of him. "You chose the wrong weapon."

Without a reply, the figure began to advance on him. He stood his ground, holding the knife still, not waving it, because that was showtime stuff. Anybody who waved a knife most likely wouldn't know how to use it.

The figure advancing on him was also holding his knife still. Apparently, he knew how to use it, which would make it interesting, but to him the outcome would be the same as it always was. After he'd taken care of his opponent, he'd go through his pockets and find out just who he was—if he had anything in his pockets. If he was a pro, he wouldn't, and he seemed to be a pro.

And then it all happened too fast for the victim to follow. He was so confident that he couldn't believe that, all of a sudden, his opponent's knife was sunk to the hilt in his stomach.

How could that have happened, he asked himself as he fell to the wet pavement. As the cold ground kissed his cheek, and a blazing fire filled his gut, he thought, So this is how they felt, all those others, this is how they felt when they were dying, with his knife in their gut. . . .

If he had known it was this bad, if he had only known this was how they felt, he would have been more compassionate. . . .

. . . damn, it hurt. . . .

. . . this was what it felt like . . . to die. . . .

. . . shit. . . .

The killer collected the balance of the fee for the twenty-fourth victim beneath a bridge in one of the largest cities in the world. Again, it was dark, for the killer only existed in darkness. All of the killings were done in the dark, as were all of the negotiations.

This one was no different.

"We have another," said the other person as he handed over the remainder of the money, "at twice your normal rate."

Neither person could see the other's face. They were like two disembodied voices carrying on a conversation.

The client's voice was flat, without inflection or distinguishable accent. It had taken him years of practice to get his voice just that way.

The killer's voice was a low rasp, clearly an attempt at disguising its true tone. Identification from that voice would be impossible with a voice print.

"What is the name?" the killer asked. "What is so special about this one that you are willing to pay double?"

The pronunciation of each and every syllable was also at attempt at disguising his voice.

"I don't think you've ever faced anyone quite like this one before," the client explained.

The killer put the money in a pocket and said, "They are all the same, and they all end up the same."

"Not this one," the client disagreed. "We want this one to be as violent as possible, and we want it known that you were the one who did it."

"What's the name?" the killer asked impatiently.

"Just as you are the best at what you do, so is he the best at what he does. He has been at this game a long time—longer than you—and he has an impeccable record and reputation. He's broken up more of our operations than we care to admit. We want him out of the way, for good, and we don't want it to look like an accident. We want it to look like someone got him out of the way, permanently."

The killer was starting to get excited. Something special for victim number twenty-five; that was very appealing. The last five had been easy, much too easy, including the last, which had been a disappointment. That man had also had a reputation but had not quite lived up to it.

A challenge was just what the killer needed, something special.

The killer was more than just a hit man. That's all most of them were, hit men. This one, however, was an artist, and as such would accept nothing short of perfection. When that knife had sunk to the hilt in the stomach of victim number twenty-four, that had been perfection.

A challenge such as victim number twenty-five would be something very, very special.

"All right," the killer said, "who is it?"

The killer could feel the dramatic pause that the other man was using to set up the final revelation. When it finally came, however, it was worth the wait.

"Nick Carter," said the client. "The name is Nick Carter."

The killer had been right. This was perfect, but not only that, it was special—which was only fitting, since the killer was known throughout the espionage world as the Specialist.

And the Specialist vs. the Killmaster—well, that was very special indeed.

CHAPTER ONE
Four Years Ago

"Another new record," the timekeeper announced after I'd finished my run through the AXE obstacle course.

Acutally, it wasn't exclusively an AXE course. I mean, one of our people had designed it, but it was made available to all government agencies for training of new agents and the retraining of older ones. For me, however, this was just a workout. As I did every year—without blowing my own horn, of course—I had just set a new course record, breaking my own previous one.

Big deal.

"Fine," I told the timekeeper, Adams, who was also the course director, or some such title. I honestly didn't think about things like records while working the obstacle course. If I happened to set a new one, hey, that was fine, but that wasn't in my mind as I was going through it.

I ejected the empty clip from the course weapon and returned both pieces to Adams for him to reload and give to the next agent.

What *was* on my mind at the moment was a blonde.

There were several other agents waiting their turns to go through the course, and the blonde was one of them. She was young, perhaps even as young as twenty, and she was very pretty. She stood very confidently, waiting her turn. About five-four, slim, with high, proud, young breasts and long legs.

I was very interested in how she would do, so I stepped to the sidelines and watched as Adams handed her the now reloaded weapon, which looked too big for her hand.

She checked the weapon before signaling to Adams that she was ready.

He gave her the signal, and she was off.

The course is a mock battlefield, but not the kind of battlefield that armies fight on. It's the kind of battlefield that field agents usually encounter. It's made up of doorways and alleys, with pasteboard opponents. As you fire, your hits are electronically scored, as are the hits on the agents if they fail to avoid any.

She went through the course steadily, confidently, missing only one shot and avoiding all enemy attempts on herself. She had run an excellent score, the best I'd ever seen, other than my own. To date, I was the only one who ever ran the entire course without missing a shot and without being hit.

She had come damned close to being the second, and I knew why she had missed the shot.

When she was through she handed the weapon back to Adams, shaking her head. Adams was shaking his, too. He had never seen a woman run up such a score. Apparently, she was displeased with her showing.

I approached her and said, "Very impressive."

Indicating the gun, which was now being reloaded for the next agent, she said, "The balance was off. I shouldn't have missed that shot."

Again, I was impressed with her. I, too had noticed that the weapon's balance was off, but I had compensated for it. I knew that was why she had missed that shot.

"You should have compensated for that," I told her.

She looked at me sharply, then nodded slowly, realizing the truth of what I had said. "You're right, I should have. You're Nick Carter, aren't you?"

"I'm flattered," I said. "And your name is. . .?"

"Laurence, Casey Laurence. I've heard quite a bit about you during training. Is it possible that it could all be true?"

"Possible," I admitted, laughing, "but not probable. How new are you?"

She shrugged.

"I guess you could call this graduation," she admitted.

"What branch?" I asked. She told me and I nodded. She would be working for one of the more active operational branches of the government's secret services.

Indicating the course, I said, "If you can keep cool the way you did out there, you should maintain a high safety factor—as long as you know when to quit."

"And do you?" she asked.

I laughed again.

"I should have quit a long time ago," I admitted. "My safety factor is nil."

"Ah, but then again, you're Nick Carter," she reminded me. "You make your own safety factor, don't you?"

"I try to," I replied, vowing to find out what they were telling these kids about me in training. "Why don't you let me take you to dinner tonight—as a graduation present?"

She was about to answer when a tall young man approached, interrupting her.

He was taller than I was, and slimmer. He moved with the easy grace of a natural athlete, but the look on his face was cocky, arrogant, and I knew what was coming.

Was I that arrogant at that age? An arrogance that

projected itself even before he spoke?

"Great show, Casey. Don't you think so, pop?"

"Allan, I'd like you to meet Nick Carter," Casey introduced. "Nick, this is Allan Trumball. He's also graduating today."

"Well, well," Trumball said, standing back and looking me up and down, "the immortal Nick Carter. You keep yourself in pretty good shape for a guy your age, don't you, Carter?"

I ignored him, which probably pissed him off, and asked Casey, "What about tonight?"

"Hey, Casey, I thought we were going out tonight?" Trumball interjected.

"You thought so, Allan," she told him, "but I never agreed."

"You're not going out with him, are you?" he asked. Then he turned to me and added, "No offense, Carter, but tonight she needs to be with someone her own age, you know?" Winking he went on, "She's a little young for you, don't you think? You might not be able to handle her."

Casey planted her fists firmly on her hips and said to him, "And you think you can? Aren't you overestimating yourself a little, Allan?"

"I don't think so," he said defensively. "I could handle you better than this old-timer could."

Now, I'm not an easy man to ruffle, and it would take more than this brash young braggart to do so, but I decided to teach him a little lesson in humility for his own good. Confidence was fine, but overconfidence made for a short career in this business.

"Trumball!" Adams called. "You're up!"

Trumball turned and signaled that he had heard. Then he turned back to me and said, "Watch this, pop."

"You know," I called out, catching him before he could rush off, "this course, as good as it is, doesn't quite prepare you for the real thing. There's no real pressure out there, aside from beating the clock, and failing that doesn't really cost you anything."

"What are you proposing?" he asked.

"Just this: Let's go through the course together. You know, we'll put a friendly little wager on it."

"What's the bet?" he asked, obviously unable to believe his luck. He would not only get to show up the great, over-the-hill Nick Carter, but he'd get to do it in front of Casey, who I suspected he'd been after all through training and had not been able to get to first base with. She hadn't been receptive to him up until now, but he felt sure she would after this.

"How about dinner tonight, with Casey, on the loser?" I proposed. Then before she could get offended at being offered up as the prize, I turned to her and asked, "Would you mind setting yourself up as the victor's spoils?"

And I had been right. She had been about to object, but since I had done the gentlemanly thing and asked her permission, she decided to consent.

"No, not at all."

"Good." To Trumball I said, "Shall we go?"

"Age before perfection," he replied.

I approached Adams and told him that Trumball and I were going through the course together. He rolled his eyes and went for another gun, which he handed to me. I hefted it and found that it was perfectly balanced. I offered to trade weapons with Trumball.

"The balance is bad on yours," I told him.

Naturally, he didn't believe me.

"I'll stick with this one."

I shrugged and said, "Suit yourself."

"I always do."

We set up at the starting line, and when we were both ready, I gave Adams the go-ahead.

"Go!" he barked.

As soon as we started I began to lecture him, putting the pressure on.

"Now, you've got to use your eyes at all times, son. Using your peripheral vision is very important if you want to stay alive . . ." He snapped off a hasty shot, and I said, "There, you see? You almost missed that one . . . don't hold your gun so tightly, it has to be able to move easily . . . hold it too tight and your hand starts to perspire . . . you lose control that way . . . your gun is like a woman, kid, treat her right and she'll treat you right . . . and keep your balance, keep your feet firmly planted, but be flexible . . . your own balance is very important . . . oops, see, that's one hit on you . . ."

By the time he had completed the course he was covered with perspiration. I knew I had gone through perfectly, but he had missed several shots and had been hit a couple of times.   He was good; there was no doubt in my mind about that. He had the raw talent, but until he learned a little humility he was going to be a liability to anyone he worked with.

Adams approached me and said, "No new record this time, Nick."

"I was handicapped," I told him, ejecting the clip from my weapon and handing him both pieces.

To Trumball he said, "You were killed three separate times, Trumball. You'll have to go through again before I can pass you."

Trumball cursed and pushed his weapon into Adams's hand.

"The goddamned thing is off balance," he told him.

"You should have compensated," Adams told him. In fact, several of the course weapons were badly balanced, some worse than others, but that was all part of the course.

"I told you the balance was off," I reminded him.

"And I was supposed to believe you!" he spat.

"It turns out you should have." I leaned toward him and tapped him on the chest with my finger, once. "I'm not your enemy, son," I told him. "You had better learn to tell the difference. Between friends, enemies . . . and 'tweeners."

A 'tweener was an in-betweener, which is where he and I were right now. I hoped it would stay that way.

"Screw you!" he snapped.

Casey approached us and asked me, "What time will you pick me up, Nick?"

"How does eight sound?"

"That sounds fine. Let's go someplace . . . expensive, okay?" she asked, catching Trumball's eye.

"Screw the both of you!" Trumball spat. He headed for the course starting line again, then turned and called out, "I won't forget this, Carter!"

"I hope not," I called after him, "because you'll be getting the bill for dinner."

He cursed again and stalked off. If he didn't cool down, he was going to blow the course the second time through, too.

"He's a very sore loser," Casey informed me.

"I'd be, too," I told her. "Look at the prize he lost."

She smiled shyly, looking even younger than she was, and touched my arm lightly.

"I'm looking forward to tonight," she told me.

"I'll try not to be too much of a disappointment to you," I promised.

"I doubt that you could be," she said. "I doubt it very much."

CHAPTER TWO

At the obstacle course Casey had been wearing basic black: black pants, black turtleneck sweater, black boots. When I picked her up that night she answered the door wearing designer jeans and an orange blouse with a matching neckerchief. The blouse was open at the neck, as were a couple of buttons further down, revealing the swell of her high, young breasts. Her boots were brown leather, and the designer jeans were blue. Her top was very sheer, and it was obvious that she was not wearing a bra.

Her nipples were rather large, that much I could tell, but their color was indiscernible, which only told me that they weren't penny brown. That would have been very obvious through the sheerness of the blouse. No, I could only believe that they were that gentle shade of coral pink that most blondes had.

I was struck once again by how very young she looked when she opened the door to her apartment. Her hair was very clean and fragrant, and it hung down to her shoulders in shimmering waves.

"It's too bad," I commented.

"What is?" she asked, her blue eyes narrowing.

"Your hair."

"What about it?" She touched it as we spoke.

"Well, it's lovely, it really is, but you'll have to cut it."

"Why?" She clutched at it protectively.

I touched it myself and told her, "In the field it will be more of a liability than anything else."

"I guess you're right," she agreed, obviously never having given it any thought until I mentioned it.

Remiss of her instructors.

I touched her hair gently, caressing it, letting it tickle the palm of my hand.

"For tonight, however," I assured her, "it's fine, just fine."

She took my hand in her hand and, holding it tightly, stepped out into the hall with me, closing her apartment door firmly behind her.

If she had any intention of inviting me into her apartment, it would be after dinner.

Practical girl.

"Where are we going?" she asked.

"You said someplace expensive, but . . ." I trailed off, indicating her jeans. I was not at all sure that they were appropriate attire for the restaurant I had in mind.

"Don't be an old fogey, Nick. Jeans are in—they're accepted dress for almost anywhere."

I conceded the point.

"Okay, if you say so."

We went out to my rented car, and I was feeling a little self-conscious about the conservative cut of my suit. I was usually in vogue when it came to new fashions, but I couldn't figure out when I had let myself fall out of touch.

Was I getting old?

Silly question. Everyone gets old, but was I *really* getting old?

Not if I could help it.

At dinner I attempted to get to know her a little better, while keeping myself a virtual mystery to her. It was a habit I could not break, not even with a fellow government worker.

She was from the midwest and had finished college at nineteen. She had been undecided about a career in journalism or photography, so she had been prime for a government recruiter. On the basis of her college records, they had recruited her right out of school, and she had been just undecided enough to say yes.

And here she was.

"And what about you?" she asked.

"What about me?"

"How did you get in this business?"

I shrugged and sipped my wine.

"It's been so long," I told her. "It seems to me that I've always been in this business. I'm good at it."

"At killing, you mean?"

"There's more to it than just that," I told her. "I'm good at all of it. I always have been."

"All of those Nick Carter stories that they tell us in training—" she began.

I waved her off.

"I'll have to talk to them about that. Those stories are what put young agents like Allan Trumball on my case. They take it as a challenge. Those stories are going to get some young agents killed."

"But are they true?" she insisted on knowing.

"I don't know exactly what you're being told," I admitted, "but I would suspect that the stories are overly exaggerated. Let's just leave it at that, okay? More wine?"

"I'd love some more wine," she said, extending her glass. "After all, this is a celebration, isn't it? The dinner was lovely, Nick. Thank you."

"I'm glad you approved."

"And I don't stand out like a sore thumb in my jeans after all, do I?" she asked.

I looked around the dining room and, just at a casual glance, saw two or three other women wearing jeans.

"No, I guess you don't. You do stand out, but it certainly has nothing to do with the way you're dressed."

"Why, thank you, sir."

We clinked glasses and drank.

"Nick?"

"Yes?"

"I think I'd like to go back to my apartment now," she told me, her eyes catching mine. The meaning was clear.

"All right."

I signaled for the check and paid it, tipping generously. After all, it wasn't my money.

During the drive back to her place she was very quiet. Her hand was on my knee the whole way, and I could feel the tension in her body.

Once we entered her apartment she showed me how truly impatient she was. She turned and fit easily into my arms, her mouth grinding hungrily against mine. I could taste the wine she had drunk, but it couldn't disguise the natural sweetness of her lips.

Her tongue was alive in my mouth, searching for mine. I broke the kiss abruptly and held her at arm's length. I unbuttoned her blouse the rest of the way, bringing surprisingly ample breasts into view. Dressed, she was deceptive, seeming slimmer than she actually was.

I removed the blouse and rubbed my palms against her nipples, which were indeed pink, bringing them to life. Then I cupped her breasts in my hands, and she closed her eyes, surrendering herself to the sensations.

I had her naked very quickly, and followed suit. Then I lifted her in my arms, finding once again that she was deceptively heavy. I enjoyed the way her smooth, warm skin felt against mine. I carried her to the bedroom under her directions, which were murmured with her mouth once again against mine. I set her down gently on the bed, and then joined her.

"Oh, Nick," she breathed as my lips found her smooth breasts and hard nipples. I kissed and nibbled them while she held my head, crushing my face against her. While my mouth worked there, my hands roamed elsewhere as I sought to familiarize myself with her body.

Soon my mouth was working its way down, pausing at her puckered navel and at the slight swell of her belly.

"Now, Nick, do it now," she pleaded. "We'll go slower next time, darling, but I need it now!"

I was happy to oblige her.

I raised myself above her and slid easily into her warm, slick depths. Her legs wrapped themselves around me, and her nails raked my back.

"Nick, Nick," she whispered, as our tempo increased, and we found the perfect rhythm, until together we reached that point of no return that all lovers seek desperately and then, once found, regret having discovered so soon.

CHAPTER THREE

"Nick?"

"Hmm?"

"Have you ever thought about . . . free-lancing?"

"No."

"Just like that, without even thinking about it?" she asked, rubbing her hand in a circular motion over my belly.

"I don't have to think about it," I told her.

"What about the money a man of your talents could make?"

"Which talents are you referring to?" I asked, reaching over and cupping her right breast in my hand.

"Not that, silly—although I'm sure you could probably make a bundle doing this, too," she admitted, sighing as I tweaked her nipple. "But, no, I mean your other talents."

"Like killing, for one?"

"For one."

Those stories again.

"You're talking about hiring myself out as a professional killer, a hit man for hire?"

"Not really—well, yes, maybe I am. Or maybe I mean—"

"A soldier of fortune?"

"I guess."

I frowned, wondering where this line of questioning had sprung from.

"Are you recruiting me?" I asked her.

"Don't be an ass," she said, slapping me on the stomach, "of course not. Someone in training was talking about using his training and going into business for himself."

"Hmm, not very patriotic of him, was it?"

"I guess you know who I'm talking about, huh?"

"Allan Trumball?"

She nodded her head.

"He's got a lot to learn before he can even think about something like that," I told her. More and more Allan Trumball was starting to sound like someone who was not long for this business—or, for that matter, this world.

"He doesn't agree. Unless he learned something today, he thinks he's superspy and Casanova all rolled into one."

"I hope he did learn something, for his own good," I told her sincerely.

"I doubt it. Allan came into training with a superiority complex. He took to it right away and finished right at the top of the class," she explained.

"Where'd you finish?"

She smiled.

"Just ahead of him."

"He was second?" I guessed.

She nodded.

"I was first," she confessed.

"That's pretty good. What do you think about the

possibility of going into business for *yourself*?" I asked, putting the same question to her.

She shrugged. "I haven't really thought about it, as far as I was concerned. I think maybe I'm too patriotic for that—or maybe just too chicken. Besides, I don't intend to make a career out of any of this. I'm going to get out long before my safety factor starts to shrink drastically."

"Back to photography or journalism?"

"Or something. I don't think I'm really cut out for this stuff."

"What about marriage?"

"Are you proposing?"

"Not until I find out what kind of a cook you are," I told her. "No, I was just asking."

"Well, I don't think I'm really cut out for that, either," she answered. "I'm too much of an individual. I don't think I'd be able to think for two."

"Well, from what I've seen, Casey, you're very good, but now that I've gotten to know you a little better, I think you're right. I don't think you're cut out for this life."

I began to knead both of her breasts with my hands, bringing the nipples back to their former hardness. She began to writhe beneath my touch, grinding her little bottom into the bed.

"How old are you?" I asked, suddenly very interested in knowing her exact age.

"What—what has that got to do—with anything?" she asked, her eyes closed once again. She caught her bottom lip between her teeth as I began to massage her a bit harder.

"Just asking, again."

"I'm twenty."

So young, I thought, as my mouth replaced my hands

and I rolled on top of her once more.

"Slower this time, Nick," she breathed in my ear. "Make it last this time. Make it last!"

CHAPTER FOUR
The Present

My foot was killing me.

Considering that I picked up a bullet in it on my last assignment, not to mention twisting my damned ankle almost to the point of breaking it, that was quite understandable.

"It looks good," the doctor said as he removed the dressing.

The hole was about an inch or so above my toes, crusted now with dried blood and bruised around the edges from the impact of the bullet. There was another hole on the bottom of my foot, where the bullet had exited.

"You're extremely lucky that the bullet was of a small caliber," the doctor told me. It figured to be, since it had been fired by a woman, but I didn't tell him that. I allowed him to continue uninterrupted.

"The X rays show that it didn't hit anything vital. A larger caliber and it might have ripped part of your foot away. As it is, there shouldn't be any permanent damage. It'll be sore for a few months, but that should be all. It's only been three days, but already you can move your toes. That's good."

I wiggled my toes just to prove he was right. It hurt.

"Now, the ankle—it's just a sprain, but it's a bad one. I'll bind the whole foot both to support the ankle and prevent the wound from bleeding—which it shouldn't do, providing you stay off it."

He put on the new, supportive dressing and pronounced that in a couple of months I'd be as good as new.

"Luckily, you're young," he added, then he turned and took his sixty-plus carcass to see his next patient.

To him I was young, but a few years ago I would have come through a similar experience with just a few bruises. Instead, through carelessness or just a momentary lapse, I had messed up my foot and ankle, which would take God-knew-how-long to heal and heal properly.

I was reclining in my bed in a Washington, D.C., medical facility renowned for its security, where they wouldn't ask me how I had come to receive such injuries, thinking back over the events of the past few days.

It had definitely been carelessness on my part that had put me there.

Was I slowing down?

The hell with that! So I got caught looking the wrong way just once. That didn't necessarily mean I was over the hill. You were only over the hill if you let yourself be.

And I had no intention of doing that.

"Can I get you anything, Mr. Carter?" my nurse asked, popping her head in the doorway.

"Yes, as a matter of fact, you can."

"What?"

"You can get the rest of yourself in here," I told her.

She smiled, which lit up her pretty young face, and stepped into the room.

She was about twenty-two, dark-haired, and full-figured, a figure that her severe, starched whites could not hide. Her white stockings and white shoes, which could make the best legs look like white posts, could not hide the lovely curve of her calves and ankles.

"I feel better already."

She smiled again and said, purely in jest, "Mr. Carter, you're just a dirty old man."

"Thanks loads," I said, pretending I was hurt.

She went on about her rounds, promising to stop in again.

In direct defiance of the doctor's orders, I slid off the bed and began walking, gingerly at first, then allowing more weight on the injured foot.

"Are you supposed to be doing that?" a familiar voice asked from behind me.

"Only if I ever want to walk again," I answered.

I turned around and found David Hawk, the head man at AXE, standing in the doorway; tall, gaunt, authoritative.

"Well, hobble back over to the bed so we can talk," he told me. I did so, trying my best not to hobble, and settled myself back on the bed. My ankle was throbbing, but I ignored it.

"This is an unexpected pleasure," I told Hawk. The head of AXE did not make a habit of visiting convalescing agents. They were of no use to him until they were back on their feet, ready to go to work, and then they visited him, not vice versa.

This was a very odd occurrence indeed.

"How are you feeling, N3?" he asked.

There was no danger in Hawk's using my code name,

as the medical facility we were in was a top clearance facility.

"Fine, sir, just fine. I'll be back on my feet in no time at all."

"Well, that's very good to hear, since I may have something for you within the next two weeks."

"Is that a fact?"

"It is. In fact, it's all set up. The doctor tells me that it will be some time before you're fully mobile. Some months, in fact."

"Weeks," I corrected.

Hawk frowned at that.

"I'm quite sure he said months," he said, thinking back, searching his memory for a possible flaw.

"He probably did," I admitted to save him the worry, "but I say weeks. Who are you going to believe?"

"At this point, I will not choose who to believe or who to disbelieve," he told me. "The matter will resolve itself soon enough. In any case, in two weeks time you will be flying to Pleasure Island."

"The fun-in-the-sun island in the Caribbean?"

"That's the one."

"What do we have going down there?"

"We," Hawk said, meaning AXE, "do not have anything operating there, but another government agency has, and they've requested that we lend you to them for this particular operation."

"Lend me to them?" I asked, puzzled. It had never been AXE policy to lend out its personnel, not without a fight, anyway.

"They want us to send you in as backup for two of their young agents."

"I'm supposed to babysit?" I asked incredulously. A Killmaster on a babysitting assignment?

"That is correct, N3," he replied formally. "This is

not a Killmaster operation, but then you are not in any shape for such an assignment, are you? On Pleasure Island you will very likely have nothing to do but observe."

"Sir," I said, trying to hold my temper, "isn't this just a bit uncommon?"

He cocked his head and said, "Yes, I believe it is."

"Well?"

"Well what, N3?"

"Don't I get an explanation?"

"Are you suggesting that I develop the habit of clearing all of my decisions with you?" he asked stiffly.

He was going to be stubborn about it.

"No, sir, I didn't mean to imply—"

"Am I then to understand that you intend to refuse this assignment?" he asked further.

"No, sir, that's not what I mean. You know I don't ordinarily refuse assignments, but—"

"Very well, then," he said as if the matter were settled, "in two weeks—ten days, if you can be ready by then—you may pick up your tickets at my office. You will fly to Pleasure Island where you will establish a cover as a vacationer. Choose your own profession for this cover, whatever you will be most comfortable with. The two agents you are to meet down there will explain the assignment to you in detail."

"How will I know them?" I asked resignedly.

"They will know you. When they are ready, they will make their identities known to you in such a way that you will not be able to mistake them. Until then, treat the time as sort of a vacation."

Now, that remark was the oddest of all. Hawk was not a man who was free with vacations, and for him to tell me to treat any portion of an assignment as one— well, that was just damned strange!

There was something going on down there, and I

didn't like being in the dark, but Hawk usually had good reasons for his actions. I had learned long ago to trust this man—who was my immediate superior—implicitly, no matter how difficult it might be.

This, however, was very near to stretching my resolve.

"Now," Hawk continued, "although you will not be the agent-in-charge, and this is not an AXE operation, I would nevertheless like you to maintain contact with me on a regular basis. Is that understood?"

None of this really was, but I said yes.

"Excellent."

Hawk rose from his chair and said, "Well, carry on with your self-imposed exercises, N3, if you want to make a liar out of the doctor. God knows, they're a pessimistic lot at best. I'll see you in about ten days."

"Yes, sir."

When he was gone I hobbled over to the window and watched him enter his car, which was waiting with the motor running. No sooner had he closed the back door then the car sped off.

What the hell was going on?

Was this his way of phasing me out as a Killmaster?

No, that was nonsense. I had more faith in him than to think that. Besides, bum foot or not, I was still the best in the business. We both knew that.

No, something was happening here; something was going to happen on Pleasure Island. I was going to have to watch my ass very carefully, of that much I was sure. David Hawk would never tell me to spend any portion of an assignment as if it were a vacation.

That in itself was more of a warning than anything else, and I was convinced that Hawk was telling me to be careful.

I was going into this assignment knowing full well that I wasn't being told everything.

Well, it wouldn't really be the first time, would it?

CHAPTER FIVE

I arrived at Pleasure Island twelve days later and registered under the name Nick Collins. The cover I had chosen for myself was that of a college professor who had suffered a small accident at the hands of a student on a motorcycle. Ostensibly, I had come to Pleasure Island to relax, recover, and gamble.

When I arrived I was walking with the use of a cane, which was just a little more for show than it was for necessity. My ankle was taped pretty well, and the dried scabs had fallen off my wounds. I had pretty much gotten used to the pain. The pills the doctor had given me would help alleviate the pain if it got too bad—if I had kept them. I had flushed them down the toilet as soon as I was discharged from the hospital. I was never much for relying on drugs, not even to cure my ills.

I could get around without the cane, should the need arise, but it was as much a part of my cover as was my title, Professor Nick Collins.

When I was signing in I checked out the lobby, just out of force of habit. No familiar faces, friend or enemy. That had been known to happen and blow a whole assignment before it even got started. Friends can blow a cover just as quickly as enemies can.

I allowed a bellboy to carry my bag to my room, as

part of the façade of the injured professor. When he had demonstrated how the faucets worked, and the difficulty factor of opening and closing the windows, I tipped him generously.

"Thank you, sir," he said. He was about twenty-eight, dark-haired, and blue-eyed, not too tall but very skinny.

"Is there anything else I can get you?" he asked.

"Not at the moment."

"Well, if ya need anything, just pick up the phone and ask for Al Nuss. That's me," he added unnecessarily.

"I'll let you know, Al. Thanks."

"No problem."

As he was very obviously a New Yorker, I wondered what the hell an Al Nuss was doing as a bellboy on Pleasure Island.

When he left I threw the heavy, blackthorn cane down on the bed and sat down next to it. I removed my right shoe and sock and began to massage my ankle. There was a dull throb that I knew would escalate the longer I stayed on the foot, and if I had kept the pills I might have even had a momentary thought about taking one, but drugs dulled your senses, and in my business, that could be fatal. Pain kept you awake and aware, so I decided to take a shower and then go down to the casino before having dinner.

I spent some time at the blackjack table first, playing steadily and winning a little. I took my winnings from there, however, and blew almost all of it at the crap table. Then I went to the roulette wheel and built them back up to the same point again. A little ahead once again, I decided to brave the poker table.

There were five at the table when I arrived, not counting the dealer. One of the players in particular caught my eye; a lovely, dark-haired woman of about thirty-four or so. She was the only female at the table, but she would have caught my eye in a crowd of women. She wore a low-cut blue dress, which showed off the fullness of her breasts and the dark, sensuous cleft between them.

Her eyes were large and brown and studied me, either sizing me up as an opponent or as a man. I was sizing her up, too, but not as a poker player.

I was only playing for a short time when *the* hand started to develop. *The* hand is that hand that all poker players look for during the course of the game, the one that will decide whether they will be winners or losers.

This was it.

The dealer dealt the cards out for seven card stud: two face down and one face up. My card was a black king. The lady showed an ace of diamonds. She bet twenty bucks, and I called. The other players, two to my left and two to my right, all with lower face cards, called nevertheless.

When I paired my kings on the next card, I became boss on board. I bet fifty dollars on my pair. The two players to my left dropped out. The lady pulled a jack of diamonds to go with her ace and, smiling across the table at me, raised fifty. The last two players both had low pairs on board, but saw the handwriting on the wall and folded. I called her raise.

It was developing into an interesting hand.

My next card was a queen, matching the one I had in the hole, both of them black. The lady received a ten of diamonds, to go with the ace and the jack of the same suit. I bet fifty into the raiser, and sure enough, she raised the same amount.

I called the raise.

The dealer gave us each our sixth card.

Mine was a red three, absolutely of no use to me.

Hers was a king of diamonds, which would have helped me considerably. The gathering crowd caught their breaths collectively.

I did what no one expected of me.

I bet into the raiser when she had obviously improved her hand: a hundred bucks, even though all she needed was the queen of diamonds for a totally unbeatable hand.

When she raised and I called, everyone figured that she already had it, which made my bet a foolish move. I was showing two kings and a queen of clubs which, paired with the queen of spades I had in the hole, gave me two pair. Now, I knew—and so did she—that one of the kings I needed for a full house was sitting on her side of the table. The other one had been folded long ago by the player to my immediate left. If she had the queen of diamonds in the hole, that left me one chance for a queen high full house. Then again, if she had the queen of diamonds in the hole, a queen high full house wouldn't mean peanuts. Of course, she could have had the queen of hearts in the hole, in which case she had a straight, and a beatable one.

That made the queen of diamonds the key card. If she got it, she won. If I got it, I won.

The crowd knew most of this as the dealer tossed us our seventh card.

I bet a hundred without hesitating. An unwritten rule of poker is, whether you've got it or not, bet like you do.

The same went for raising.

She raised.

I reraised.

The crowd was puzzled.

If she was puzzled, she didn't show it. She raised me back. She had the straight, one way or another, or she was bluffing.

I called, saying, "Just so it doesn't get out of hand."

"A gentleman," she observed, smiling. She had a good voice, deep and throaty, confident, and a smile that lit the room.

"The lady needs a queen of diamonds," the dealer announced , unnecessarily.

Everyone was waiting for her to turn over her card, since the last raise had been hers.

"Don't bother," I said, then turned over the first card of the hand that I had been dealt.

The queen of diamonds.

That, with the other queen I had in the hole—the one I had on the table—and the two kings on table, gave me my full house.

Her hand was dead, ladies and gentlemen, and I was the winner.

Somebody from the crowd exclaimed, "He had her card all the time!"

"Yes," she said, turning her last card over just for fun. "He did, didn't he?"

The black queen.

She had her straight, which wasn't good enough.

"For that," she told me, staring me right in the eyes, "you at least owe me a drink."

"My pleasure," I told her. To the dealer I said, "Would you have these cashed and held at the cashier's window, please? I'll pick it up later."

"As you wish, sir." He signaled to someone to pick up the chips.

I walked around the table and extended my arm to the lady. When she rose, I saw that the rest of her body matched the fullness of her breasts, and that she was about five-eight to boot.

A sizable lady.

At the bar she ordered a brandy; I ordered Wild Turkey.

When we had our drinks in hand she said, "You play well."

"You have to have the card," I answered. Up until that hand, she had been winning and I hadn't. Now, the vice was versa.

"And you did have mine all along, didn't you, you evil man?" she asked. "Why didn't you keep raising?"

I shrugged. "No point, really. It was just a friendly game of poker."

She shook her head.

"There is no such thing as a friendly game of poker," she told me. "As a matter of fact, I don't play friendly games of any kind."

That sounded ominous, like a threat of some sort.

Or a warning.

"I'll remember that," I told her, raising my glass. We clinked and drank.

"Are you here for business or pleasure?" I asked.

"The latter . . . and I'm all business about my pleasure."

"Then you're a professional pleasure-seeker?"

She shook her head.

"The word *professional* implies that someone pays you to do something, thereby making you a professional at what you are being paid to do. The word does not apply to me, because nobody pays me money; they lose it to me."

"I stand corrected. What is it you do, besides gamble?"

"I travel and enjoy life. I've been hopelessly spoiled by two wealthy husbands—and two very healthy divorce settlements."

"Divorce? Their loss, I'm sure."

"In more ways than one."

"I'm sure."

"Thanks."

"Would you possibly be free to have dinner with me tonight?" I asked. "I really don't feel that one drink has quite made up for what I did to you."

She smiled and conceded. "I think that could be arranged. Just let me freshen up, and I'll meet you in the main dining room."

"Fine."

As she turned to leave I said, "Oh, by the way—"

"Yes?"

"What's your name?" I couldn't go on thinking of her as "the lady."

She tilted her head back and laughed. It was a nice, full-bodied laugh, just like its owner.

"Yes, that would help, wouldn't it? My name is Christine Hall."

"My name is Nick Collins."

She arched her eyebrows and said, "Somehow, I knew your name would be Nick."

"Oh?" I asked, wondering if perhaps I had inadvertently made contact with one of the agents I was supposed to meet.

Then again, Hawk had referred to them as "young."

"You look like a Nick," was all she would say, adding, "See you shortly, Nick."

I watched her walk away, admiring her legs and the sway of her hips. Maybe she was younger than she looked. Perhaps she intended to make positive contact over dinner.

Or even later.

CHAPTER SIX

It became unnecessary for contact to be formally made at dinner, or at any other time, because I recognized the two agents as soon as they entered the dining room.

I had secured a table and was waiting for Christine to arrive when I saw the blonde and the tall man enter together.

Actually, I say the blonde first, remembering her immediately, even after four years. It was Casey, the young, blonde fledgling agent I had met on the obstacle course, and seen one time after that.

She had changed some since then, but I knew her right away. She was wearing a bright yellow evening gown, cut low over her deceptive breasts, showing them off to their best advantage. Yes, they looked small, but they were deceptive; I knew that from experience. She had grown into a woman, twenty-four now, if I remembered correctly. Her face had changed a bit, too. Her cheeks had hollowed out a little, and she'd cut her hair— Carter, you prognosticator, you—but there was still some little girl left in the big blue eyes and the slightly pouty mouth.

I remembered the man, too, but with much less pleasure.

Allan Trumball, the arrogant young agent I had humiliated on the obstacle course and had never seen after that—until now.

He had also filled out, being much more muscular than he had been then. Had he grown up as well? I wondered.

I hoped he had.

They had to be the two agents I was to meet, because I didn't believe in coincidences, and their presence here wasn't making it very likely that I ever would.

Casey saw me first as they entered and started down the steps. She showed no sign of recognition at all. She turned and said something to Trumball, who looked over at me with a look of undisguised distaste.

No, he hadn't grown up at all.

The couple—and a striking young couple they made, I had to admit—were being led to a table not far from mine. I hoped they hadn't been foolish enough to specify that. Our meeting was supposed to be accidental.

They had to pass behind me to reach their table, and contact was made—literally—when Casey's elbow nudged my arm just as I was lifting my water glass.

"Oh, excuse me," she cried, grabbing a napkin from my table and attempting to dry my sleeve. "I'm so sorry. I've just taken my medication you see, and there's a 'special agent' in it that makes me unsteady for a few hours afterward. I'm so sorry, please forgive me."

"It's quite all right," I assured her. She was very good, with not a hint of recognition in her manner or speech, just the mention of the code words to officially establish contact.

"Come along, sweetheart," Allan told her, grabbing her arm. "The man forgives you."

She smiled at me wanly and explained, "My husband . . ." as Trumball pulled her away.

I wondered if one or both of them had any idea that

I would be their backup. The distaste on Trumball's face when he recognized me led me to believe that he hadn't. I couldn't tell anything from either Casey's face or her reaction, which was just as it should be.

I signaled the waiter to bring another glass of water just as Christine entered the room.

She turned heads, as Casey had done when she entered. Both of them were striking women, with Christine having just about ten years on Casey. It was very often a toss-up as to whether youth or experience was the more valuable commodity in a woman. It usually depended on the circumstances.

I rose as Christine approached, still wiping at my sleeve with the cloth npakin.

"What happened to you?" she asked as I assisted her with her chair.

"Just a slight accident. A blushing new bride bumped into my arm," I explained, indicating Casey and Trumball's table.

Christine turned and looked, and her eyes caught Casey's for a moment.

"She's very pretty," she remarked. "Are you sure it wasn't intentional?"

"Oh, I don't think so. She has an attractive young husband, as you can see."

"Oh, I don't think you have any need to worry about him. He wouldn't offer you very much competition, Nick."

Little did she know how right she was.

"Well, he's bigger than I am," I offered.

"Somehow, I don't think that would matter with a man like you," she said thoughtfully.

"Well, thank you, anyway."

"You're quite welcome."

We drank to compliments, and the waiter came with two menus.

"Since I've been here a little longer than you have, Nick, and I've eaten here every night, would you like me to recommend something?" she asked.

I picked up the menu, then dropped it without opening it.

"I'll tell you what, Christine. Why don't you just order for both of us?"

"All right." She began to inspect the menu, saying, "The filet is quite good, with a divine butter sauce."

"Sounds good."

"Then that's what we'll have."

"Would you mind if I ordered the wine?"

"Not at all."

The waiter took our orders, the menus, and then left.

I was looking at Christine through different eyes, now that I knew she wasn't my contact. She was a possible hindrance—and a possible dalliance—but then again, she would make a good addition to my cover. She was also very pleasant and beautiful, and I wouldn't mind spending some time with her one bit.

She seemed to feel the same.

This night, at least, could turn out to be something very special.

"Where did you learn to play poker?" I asked her.

"From my daddy. He was a professional gambler and taught me everything he knew—before he left my mother and me."

"You learned very well."

"It was all my daddy ever gave me," she explained. "It wasn't only cards he taught me, though. He taught me how to gamble, period—and by that I mean as a way of life. I've married twice and divorced well both times. That's two winning hands out of two."

"That's an optimistic view of marriage," I observed.

"I'm well-off enough now that I can indulge my thirst for both travel and gambling."

"Thirst?" I asked, thinking the word odd.

"Yes. Hunger is a word I reserve for . . . other pleasures," she told me with a mischievous glint in her eyes. She was transmitting and I was receiving, which was almost perfect.

I glanced over at Casey and Trumball from time to time without seeming to. I caught Trumball's eyes more than once, but never caught Casey looking my way, although I knew she was. She was very good indeed.

He still seemed to have a lot to learn, and if he hadn't in four years, I doubted very seriously he ever would.

He wouldn't live long enough to.

I wondered if they had been made a team right out of training, or if they had ever even worked together before this. I'd have to talk to Casey. If they were partners, she would have to dump him soon. Four years was a long time to carry someone before he or she finally got you killed.

"Here's dinner," Christine announced, breaking into my thoughts. "You're really going to love this sauce."

"I'm sure I will."

And I did.

We discussed our backgrounds, with me once again, as always, inventing some new story to go along with my cover—where I was born, where I grew up, and so on.

She was from Louisiana, she finally admitted, which would explain her gambling background—riverboat gamblers, and all that.

"I thought I detected some sort of accent," I told her. "You try to hide it, don't you?" I teased.

She looked embarrassed.

"If I'm going to be successful at what I do, it wouldn't be prudent for me to sound like a Mississippi gambler, now would it?" she asked.

We had finished dinner and the bottle of wine at the same time, and as I was about to signal for the waiter and order another bottle, I saw him approaching with one.

Psychic?

"I'm sorry," I told him, "We didn't—"

"The young couple, sir," he said by way of explanation. He was indicating Casey's table and added, "The Tremaynes. By way of apology, the lady said."

"I see. Thank you."

He poured, left the bottle, and vanished, the way waiters have a habit of doing in restaurants all over the world.

"See?" Christine said. "What did I tell you. No competition."

"Don't be silly," I told her. "It's perfectly innocent." I raised my glass to Casey, who raised hers back, smiling. She was playing it to the hilt, all wide-eyed and innocent.

"Sure," she drawled knowingly.

"Don't be silly," I said again.

She drained her glass and extended it for a refill, saying, "There's something I've been wanting to ask you, Nick, but I wanted to wait until I knew you better."

"Is this the time?" I asked.

"Yes."

"What is it?"

"Your foot. I thought the cane was for show, originally, but you do move rather awkwardly. What happened to it?"

I smiled and said, "It was run over by a motorcycle."

"C'mon."

"It's true," I lied. "A careless student, late for a class, zipping through campus, and a college professor looking the other way."

"At some pretty young co-ed's legs?"

"Guilty," I said, smiling again.

"I guess that means you can't dance," she observed.

"Uh, maybe something slow, if we don't move around too much," I offered.

"Then why don't you ask the young bride to dance?" I laughed.

"Why should I do that?"

"It would be your way of showing her that you forgive her, ah, clumsiness. Besides, she's obviously developed a crush on you, which could disastrous for a new bride, unless she gets you out of her system early."

"And you think that dancing with me will get me out of her system? Thanks a lot."

She touched my hand and said, "Don't tell me you've never had this problem before, not a handsome college professor like you. You must have young girls developing crushes on you all the time. How do you handle them?"

I thought a moment.

"I don't know, but if this works, I may start taking them dancing. Excuse me."

I got up and approached Casey's table, trying not to move too awkwardly.

Trumball noticed me first and leaned forward to say something to Casey. She didn't turn, however, until I called out their phony name.

"Mr. and Mrs. Tremayne?"

"Yes?" she replied, turning and smiling.

"My name is Collins, Nicholas Collins. I wanted to thank you for the wine, and also tell you that it wasn't really necessary."

"My wife was concerned that she had ruined your suit," Trumball explained.

"It was only a sleeve, and it was only water. I assure you, no harm done."

"I'm glad," Casey said.

"I thought perhaps a dance might even things up," I suggested. Turning to Trumball I added, "Would you mind?"

"Why should I?" he answered. "It's not me you want to dance with."

I groaned inwardly, but Casey picked up the ball nicely.

"I'd love to dance," she said. I put out my hand and she gave me hers. I led her to the dance floor, and she came easily into my arms. We stayed to the center of the floor, allowing the other dancers to circle around us, effectively shielding us from view. I moved my feet very little, if at all.

"After four years, I still fit pretty well, don't I?" she remarked.

"Perfectly," I replied.

Her hair smelled just as I remembered it, clean and fresh. I could feel the new fullness in parts of her body, and the new slenderness in others. She'd dropped the babyfat where she didn't need it, and filled out where she did. She did, indeed, fit very well.

"It's good to see you again, Nick. I'm surprised to see you on an assignment like this, though," she admitted.

"I hurt my ankle recently. This is kind of a working rest."

"I thought you were moving a little awkwardly."

"I left my cane at the table."

"I won't let you fall," she promised.

"Thank you."

"Was this your idea? The dance?"

"Christine's," I admitted, but it had struck me as a good way to talk to her alone, without Trumball.

"Ah, your lady friend."

"It was as good an excuse as any to get to talk to you without your, uh, husband around."

"Is she part of your cover?"

"Christine? No, I just met her tonight. I took some of her money at the poker table, and we ended up having dinner."

"Dinner . . . and—?" she asked.

"That's a possibility," I admitted.

She smiled, but it didn't seem genuine. She couldn't be jealous, could she? I mean, not after one incident that occurred four years ago.

Then again, she was a woman, wasn't she, and they usually needed very little provocation to become jealous.

"What's your cover?" she asked.

"I'm Nicholas Collins, a college professor. I'm here recovering from an injury I received when a student ran over my foot with his motorcycle."

"Accidently, I hope."

"Absolutely. He was late for class."

"That's a shame. They shouldn't allow those things on campus."

"I've told them that time and time again," I replied. "What about you and Allan? Newlyweds?"

"Very," she sighed.

"Have you worked together long?"

"Quite a few times."

"Has he grown up any?"

"I'm afraid he's still pretty much the same as he ever was," she confided. "He's still never forgiven you for what you did to him in training."

"That's his misfortune, Casey, and it may be the death of him. Don't let it be yours, too. Dump him."

"Oh, Allan's not all that bad, Nick, really. He's helped me out a few tight spots over the past few years."

"I don't doubt it, but maybe if he hadn't been there, you never would have gotten into those tight spots in the first place," I suggested.

She seemed to give that remark serious consideration before going onto the next question.

"How's your safety factor these days?"

"You've cut your hair," I observed.

"Do you like it?"

"Very much."

"I did it soon after that evening you suggested it. You were right, you know. I can think of two or three times it would have gotten in the way, had it been longer. Thanks."

"Don't mention it."

The music was ending and she asked, "Can we meet tomorrow morning? On the beach or by the pool?"

"Pick it," I told her.

"There are some tables by the beach. Have breakfast there about nine, and we'll come a little later."

"Fine."

The dance ended, and I was glad. My ankle was really starting to throb. She noticed it as we walked back to the table.

"Are you going to be all right?"

"Sure. I'll just pick up my cane, pay the check, and be off," I assured her.

"Get a good night's rest," she advised.

"I'll be in bed early," I promised.

"I know that, but I said rest," she whispered as we reached her table.

I would have goosed her for that, but it wouldn't have looked proper.

I assisted her with her chair and said, "Thank you for the dance, Mrs. Tremayne. Mr. Tremayne, enjoy your evening."

"I intend to," he replied curtly.

"Good evening," I bade them both, then hobbled back to my table and Christine.

"You should get off that foot," she advised as I sat down across from her.

I sipped my wine and answered, "I think you're right.

Do you have any suggestion as to where?" I asked, signaling for the waiter and the check.

"My room?" she said without hesitation.

I paid the tab and tipped generously.

"I may have to stay off this ankle for quite a while," I warned her.

"I should hope so," she answered.

We went to her room.

I didn't get much rest, but at least I was off my foot.

CHAPTER SEVEN

Trumball attempted to make it very clear right from the start that he was the agent-in-charge, and I was just the backup.

"In charge of what?" I asked.

"Just so you know, that's all," he added, sounding like a little boy uttering that classic comeback, "Oh, yeah?"

"Trumball, you're still just as much of an ass as you ever were," I told him.

We were all sitting at a table at beachside, enjoying early-morning Bloody Marys but not each other's company.

I had arrived first, after spending a pleasant night with Christine. She had told me that early rising wasn't one of the pleasures in life she hungered for, especially not after she'd spent a night enjoying one of the pleasures she did—hunger for, I mean.

I told her I was going to hit the beach, and that I would see her later.

There weren't too many early risers on Pleasure Island, it seemed. All of the beach tables were empty when I took one, and by the time the Tremaynes arrived about twenty minutes later, only one other was occupied.

When I'd seated myself, Al Nuss came out and bade me a good morning.

"Good morning, Al."

"What can I get for you, sir?" he asked.

"Doubling as a waiter today?"

"Extra tips," he confided. "Up late?"

I nodded.

"Feel like eating something?"

I shook my head.

"A Bloody?"

I nodded.

"Be right back."

He was. When he returned, I asked him to sit for a minute.

"You're from New York," I commented.

"You got good ears."

"You got a heavy accent," I mimicked.

"Yeah," he agreed.

"Al, are you the man around here?"

"You mean, *the* man?"

"No, I mean, can you get me something I want, when I want it?" I clarified.

"That depends on what you want," he answered shrewdly.

"Do you have limitations?" I asked as if surprised at the very thought.

"Very few. What's your story, pal?"

"I just like having you around," I told him, "in case I should need you."

He nodded thoughtfully, then rose and said, "I gotta go back to work."

"Thanks for the Bloody."

"Don't forget the tip," he reminded me, taking liberties now that we were buddies.

"I won't," I promised.

Opening up even that much to Al Nuss may have been a wrong move, but it was made on instinct, an instinct I had come to rely on very heavily during the years. I had the feeling that if I needed anything other than my personal sidearms—Wilhelmina, Hugo, and Pierre—that Al Nuss would be able to supply it.

For a New York boy to be stuck out here on Pleasure Island, he had to be running something on the side, whether it was drugs, girls . . . or something more deadly. There had to be something else in it for him, other than tips.

I hoped his presence here would turn out to be nothing more than that.

I was half done with my drink when Casey and Trumball put in their appearance.

We went through a fancy-meeting-you-here act.

I stood up and called, "Mr. and Mrs. Tremayne."

"Mr. Collins," Casey called back, waving gaily.

Trumball was going to have to do some serious work on the look that came over his face whenever he saw me. He didn't necessarily have to change it, just hide it better.

"Join me, please," I invited.

Naturally they accepted and sat with me.

Casey was wearing a one-piece bathing suit that showed just how deceptive her figure was. Her breasts, round and firm, showed clearly in the suit. Her waist was rather long, her hips slim. Long, smooth legs completed the picture.

Trumball was wearing blue bathing trunks—bikini style—and he had the build for them. He was tall, slim-waisted, and well-muscled without being muscle-bound. He had a white towel draped over his shoulders.

It was when they sat down that Allan told me that he was the boss, he was in charge, and I was just a hired hand.

That was when I told him he was an ass.

"Listen, Carter—" he snapped.

I looked away from him in total disgust. Calling an agent by his real name while running a covert operation was a mortal sin, and showed even more clearly that the man still had far too much to learn.

"He's right, Allan," Casey told him.

"What?" he asked, looking at her incredulously.

"You are an ass."

"Now, wait a minute—"

"No, you wait! First of all, you're not the agent-in-charge here, not by yourself you're not. *We* are in charge, Allan. *Together.* So get down off your high horse, damn you!" she hissed. "And don't ever call Nick anything but Mr. Collins while we're on Pleasure Island. Is that understood?"

I had a feeling that they had gone through similar scenes before. Trumball was looking properly chagrined at Casey's scolding. Casey hadn't lied to me when she said that they had worked together quite a few times. They were a permanent team, and she was the dominant member.

Casey looked at me and said, "Maybe I'd better explain what we're all doing here."

"Drinks?" Al Nuss asked.

Three superspies, right? And none of us noticed that he was approaching the table until he spoke. I wondered how much he might have heard, and how he might have interpreted it.

"I'll have another," I told him.

"Juice," Casey said. "Orange juice."

"Sir?" Al addressed Trumball.

"The same," he finally said. I could have sworn he was waiting for Casey to order for him.

"Yes, sir," Al Nuss said, then went to get the drinks.

"Okay," I told her, "let's have it."

She leaned forward and began.

"There's a house on the other side of this island, Nick. It's the only other structure on the island besides this hotel."

"A house?"

"Well, it's more like a castle, really. The man who lives there is named Oswaldo Orantes. He's very rich. As a matter of fact, he owns Pleasure Island."

"I'd say that was pretty rich, all right," I remarked, wondering where all of this was leading. "Does he own the island *and* the hotel?"

She shook her head.

"Just the island. He rents this side of the island to a syndicate of businessmen who wanted to turn it into the greatest warm weather resort in the world. Beach, pool, entertainment, and gambling."

"Orantes doesn't even have a little piece?"

"Well, he is on the board of directors, but he's really just a token member."

"Okay, so he's a rich man who owns an island and has a new toy. What else?"

"He also buys and sells information. He buys from anyone, and sells to the highest bidder."

So, now I knew where it was leading.

"Recently, he picked up some information that we'd like to get our hands on."

" 'We' meaning the United States government," I added.

"Who else?" Trumball asked.

He got dirty looks from both of us, and Casey continued.

"We discovered that he's going to play it cute this time. He's going to sell the information twice; to the opposition *and* to us. We want to grab the information before he can do that. That'll put us one up on the opposition."

"What makes you think that they're not going to do the same thing, which would put them one up on us?" I asked. "Then again, if we both buy the info, that'll keep us even. What's so bad about that?"

"You must be kidding," Trumball asked.

"Nick, we've got to be one up on them," Casey explained. "We've got to stay ahead in this game."

"This is a game?" I asked.

They both looked at me, baffled. Neither one could understand my suggestion that a stand-off was better than someone being one up. But then neither of them had been in this "game" as long as I had.

"Okay, okay, forget that. What's the information?" I asked.

"You don't need to know that," Trumball said quickly.

Casey looked at him with distaste but agreed nevertheless.

"He's right, Nick. You're our backup, in spite of who you are, and you really don't need to know that, at this point."

"Okay," I said, going along for the moment. "I'll buy that for now. Let me get this straight: you two intend to go into Orantes's mansion, grab the info, and get out again."

"Right."

"How long has this stuff been on the block?" I asked.

"It's been available for two weeks, and he's taking bids for another week," Casey answered.

"Which means that there may be some guests here at the hotel who, like us, are out to snatch the info, or are here to bid on it," I observed.

"That was something I wanted to ask you about," Casey said. "You have been around a lot longer than we have. Have you recognized anyone since you arrived here yesterday?"

"No" I answered after having searched my ancient mental file. "But that doesn't mean that there can't be enough agents in this hotel right now for us to have a convention."

"That's why you're here as a backup," she said.

"No, that's why you *need* a backup," I corrected. "That's not why I'm here as a backup. I intend to find out exactly why I'm here on this island, but that will come after we're finished. Now, how do you intend to get inside Orantes's place?"

"Not the way you think," she told me. "I wasn't kidding when I said his house was like a castle. It's virtually impenetrable."

I'd heard that before, but it was their show, so I listened.

"So, what's the plan?"

A small, coy smile crossed Casey's face as she said, "Orantes likes blondes."

"I see."

"And especially married ones," she added.

"I'm getting the picture."

"Here's the scam. Orantes gambles one night a week, here at the hotel. That's tomorrow night, Saturday. I'm going to look my absolute best—hopefully—and make myself available. Hopefully again, he'll bite. My husband will develop a headache or something, leaving me alone—and vulnerable."

"You'll go with Orantes to his house—alone—and get back out again with the dope."

"Right."

"This seems like a pretty iffy plan," I told them. "Whose idea was it?"

"Casey's," Trumball was quick to say.

"What happens if Orantes walks in with a blonde on his arm? What happens if he doesn't bite? What happens if he develops a headache? What then?"

"Then we come up with another plan," Casey said.

"You don't have a backup plan?" I asked.

"Not, uh, a thoroughly-worked-out one, no," Casey admitted.

I shook my head in disbelief.

The whole thing sounded so amateurish I wanted to laugh.

"This whole thing depends on your ability to attract Orantes?"

"So far," she admitted. "Why, don't you think I can?"

"Casey, no offense, but as lovely as you are, you are not totally irresistible."

She lowered her lashes at me, placed her elbow on the table and her chin in her hand, and said, "We'll see."

I couldn't believe she was really taking this whole thing as a challenge, a game.

Unless there was something they weren't telling me.

Which, considering the way things had been going so far, made a lot more sense then their plan.

CHAPTER EIGHT

"Allan, go for a swim," Casey suddenly told Trumball. Not "Why don't you go for a swim?" but "Go for a swim" period—as in, "That's an order!"

"Casey—" he began.

"You said you wanted to go swimming," she reminded him.

"Yeah, I know, I do, but—"

"So go. The briefing is over, and I'd like to talk to Nick alone—about old times. Ta-ta, husband."

He threw me a murderous glance, but damned if he didn't up and go for a swim, just like he was told to.

When he was gone I said, "He's your regular partner, isn't he?"

"Yes, but I can pretty much control him," she assured me.

"No wonder he's still alive. You've been keeping him that way, haven't you?"

"Now, Nick, I told you last night, it hasn't been all that one-sided a partnership. He's good at what he does. He just needs some direction, that's all."

"Direction," I repeated. "Oh, I get it. You say swim, he swims, you say kill, he kills. Is that it?"

"Not exactly."

"He's going to get you killed, Casey. Dump him, for your own good."

She placed her hand over mine.

"Do you need a partner?" she asked.

"Unfortunately, I work alone," I told her. "Otherwise, I could do worse."

"So, you see? I'll just have to stick with what I've got." She moved her hand up my arm and said, "You know, I'm glad you're here, Nick. I don't mind telling you I'm scared, even after four years in this game."

Again with the word *game*.

"Don't ever get to the point when you're not scared, Casey. That's when you get reckless. Unless you're like Trumball," I added, waving a hand at the water. "Then you start out reckless."

"He's not as bad as all that," she said again, rushing to his defense.

"Listen, are you and he, uh—"

"Close?" she asked. "Would that bother you?" She seemed delighted at the prospect.

"Not at all."

"Oh." A hint of disappointment. "Well, we're not. Although Allan would like to be. I'm just not interested in him," she explained, "that way." She leaned closer and whispered, "I've been spoiled."

"Casey, what's this information that we're after?" I asked, changing the subject.

She became serious.

"I don't know if I should, Nick. Oh, what the hell, if I can't tell you, who can I tell?" She inched her chair closer to the table. "The information has to do with germ warfare. Supposedly it's a formula and an antidote. So you see, if we both get it, it's no longer a viable weapon. We've got to get it first, Nick. My boss says it would be a major step up for us on the opposition. Don't you see?"

"Yeah, I see," I answered. "I see where that kind of thinking is taking us away from world peace, instead of toward it."

She ignored that and went on. "We're going to steal the info, but my boss had a great idea. We're going to plant some phony info in its place, hoping to set whoever gets it back a few months as well as setting ourselves ahead. Brilliant, huh?"

"That means you've got to get in and out without them knowing you did it."

"Right."

"Casey, this idea—"

"Nick, we've been here for days. I haven't seen a better-looking blonde on the island than me."

"Modesty becomes you so," I told her.

"I'm like you, Nick. I realize what I have and use it the best way I know how."

"Here comes my friend," I said, putting an end to any further conversation along those lines.

Christine was approaching, clad in a brown one-piece bathing suit with cut-out sides. She looked delicious. It's a good thing she wasn't a blonde, or that might have thrown a crimp into Casey's plan—if indeed it was Casey's plan.

"Good morning," she greeted.

I made the introductions while she took a seat, and then ordered her a Bloody Mary from Al Nuss, who gave me the fisheye because I was sitting with the two best-looking women on the island.

"How long have you been married, my dear?" Christine asked Casey.

"Just a few weeks," Casey replied.

The way she was looking at Christine reminded me very much of the way Trumball looked at me, and I didn't like it one bit. I guess there's one thing a woman can't control, no matter how much of a professional she

is, and that's jealousy. We didn't need that clouding up
the matter, and I intended to talk to Casey about it at
my earliest opportunity.

"Marriage is a wonderful institution," Christine continued. "I've tried it twice myself, with great success."

"Oh. You remarried after your first husband's
death?" Casey asked, misunderstanding Christine's remark.

"Oh, no, my dear. I'm twice-divorced, and very happily so."

Casey looked puzzled, wondering if she wasn't being
put on.

"I think I'll join Allan in the water. Thank you for the
drink, Mr. Collins."

"Nick, make it Nick, Casey," I said magnanimously.

"All right, Nick. Thank you. Have a good day, Miss
—uh, Mrs. Hall. It was a pleasure meeting you."

"Thank you, dear."

When Casey had gone down the beach, Christine said,
"Lovely child, don't you think?"

"She's not much of a child, Christine. How are you
feeling this morning?"

"Wonderful. I really enjoyed last night, Nick."

"Good, so did I."

"We'll have to do it again . . . very soon."

I had intended to keep that night open, but I didn't
think Christine was thinking quite that far in advance.

An afternoon matinee did not seem like such a bad
idea, at that.

Over an ersatz breakfast—i.e., more Bloody Marys—
I discovered something else about Christine I liked. It
became clear that she was not the kind of woman who
thought that one night in bed did a lasting relationship
make. In other words, there was none of that morning-
after drivel. In fact, after breakfast she went her own
way, not even mentioning anything about having lunch

together. That suited me fine, since I wanted to take a look at the island.

Again, though, I really wouldn't have minded a matinee.

Oh, well. . . .

CHAPTER NINE

I rented a late-model Toyota and obtained a map of the island from the desk clerk. I went back to my room and spread the map on the bed. Outlined in red was Orantes's house and grounds, and red meant OFF LIMITS.

I changed into jeans and a pair of stiff boots that offered my ankle some support. I put on a windbreaker so I'd be able to keep Hugo strapped to my wrist and Wilhelmina tucked into the rear waistband of my pants. As always, Pierre was taped to my inner thigh. All I needed was my cane, and I was off.

According to the map, there were a number of back roads that led to small clearings and ponds, ideal spots for a picnic or a romantic rendezvous. I stuck to the main highway, and found that many of these back roads were no more than footpaths, barely large enough to accommodate a vehicle.

The main road virtually circled the entire island and ran along the water—at water level in some spots, well above it in others. I was content to drive around the whole island until I reached the home of Oswaldo Orantes.

Imposing was a lame word for it. At first sight it actually did appear to be a castle, missing only a moat. It was situated atop a hill, and between it and the hotel was another large hill. I could see the roof and a couple of the top floors of the hotel from where I was. The only way you would be able to see the house from the hotel would be from one of those floors or from the roof. I wondered how many guests at the hotel were totally unaware of the house on the other end of the island.

I left the car on the side of the road, not wanting the motor to attract attention, and continued on foot as best I could. Actually, my ankle felt pretty good that day, so I decided I would take a shot at climbing the hill—with the aid of my cane—and get a closer look at the house.

Making good use of the cane I made my way up the hill until I could see the outer wall surrounding the house. That section of the wall was well hidden from the road by overgrowths of foliage, but I wasn't surprised to find such a wall. Knowing what little I did of Orantes, I would have expected some kind of security measure. In fact, if I followed the wall around to the front gate, I expected to find at least two guards on duty.

I approached the wall and leaned against it. It was at least eight to ten feet high, and probably wide enough on top for a man to walk comfortably. There were no wires that I could see on the top, barbed or otherwise. I wondered if there were any jagged materials imbedded in the top to surprise unwanted guests.

For Casey to be convinced that this place was impenetrable, there had to be more than I was seeing. More than likely, there were electric eye cells in the wall, and some kind of radar scan of the grounds, perhaps even of the outside, but that I doubted. With a resort hotel on the island, there would be too many people exploring the island for them to worry about someone outside the grounds. No, they would only be concerned with somebody on the inside who didn't belong.

Just as an experiment, I walked along the wall for

about a hundred yards or so, and did not encounter an entrance or a break of any kind. The road I had left the car on would wind around the grounds and would very likely lead right past the front gate. Perhaps that front gate was the only way in—and out.

Eventually my leg began to tire, and my ankle began to throb. I bent over to massage the ankle as best I could through my boot, and by doing so saved my life—or at least I thought I did, at the time.

In any case, I didn't hear the shot, but I didn't have to hear it to know that I had been shot at. The bullet whizzed over my head and struck the wall with a puff of dust and stone. I threw myself aside and in doing so wrenched my injured ankle, but I succeeded in avoiding the second bullet as well.

Trying to ignore the pain in my ankle, I began to run down the hill diagonally, proceeding with extreme caution to my rented car. I had Wilhelmina in my hand by then, but I had nothing to shoot at. Whoever was firing at me was doing so from a great distance, very likely with a rifle and telescopic sight.

I reached my car without a third shot having been fired. Apparently, whoever the marksman was did not think it wise to fire again after two near misses. Either that, or he or she was interrupted. Whichever it was, I was just glad the firing had stopped.

I practically fell into my car and grabbed hold of my ankle. I massaged it as best I could and then, satisfied that my foot wasn't about to fall off, abandoned it in favor of getting the hell away from there.

I made a U-turn and retraced my route back to the hotel without incident. I turned the car back in and told the attendant that, yes, it had been a pleasant ride, thank you.

My first impulse was to go straight to the roof, but the marksman—or woman—would be long gone by now, and my second impulse appealed to me a lot more: get off my foot!

I went straight to my room and removed my boot—very gingerly. I'm no doctor, but my ankle felt hot to the touch. I had no idea what that meant, but I decided to soak the damned thing. It had already begun to swell. I seemed to remember that warm water helped swelling to go down.

Or was that cold?

Then I thought of Al Nuss.

I called room service and asked for Al. When he came on the line I said, "Can you get me a doctor—"

"Sure," he answered before I had finished.

"—who won't ask questions?" I went on.

He paused a moment, then said, "Oh. Yeah, I can, but it'll cost you."

"What else is new? Get him up here, will you? And come up with him?"

"Be right there," he promised.

Maybe I was about to find out how really handy Al Nuss was going to be to me

Or maybe I was in for a surprise.

He didn't necessarily have to be more than he seemed; it was just a feeling, or rather, my instinct at work again. He could very well have just been a city dog trying to grab a way to make a fast buck.

Or he could have been much, much more than even I imagined he was.

I figured that I was probably about to find out.

CHAPTER TEN

I grabbed a quick shower and was out and dressed again by the time they knocked on the door.

I opened it and found Al and a tall, gray-haired gentleman with a black doctor's bag standing there.

"Come on in."

The doctor wasted no time earning his considerable fee, which had not yet been quoted, but which I was sure would be substantial once he saw the old bullet wounds on my foot.

"Sit on the bed, please," he instructed.

I sat and he further instructed me to remove my shoe. I removed my slipper and extended my foot for his inspection.

The bullet wound was still flaming red and unmistakable. He looked at it, then looked up at me and said, "But, this is a—"

"Al," I called out.

"Doc," Nuss told him warningly.

The doctor bit his tongue but couldn't resist peeking for the exit wound on the bottom of my foot. I let him have his peek.

"Where's the problem?" he asked.

"My ankle. I think I aggravated an old injury."

He probed at my ankle with thick finger pads, rotated

63

my foot, and asked me if that hurt.

"Hell, yes."

"It's swollen," he told me, "but there doesn't seem to be any serious damage. I'll leave you some liniment. Soak the ankle in hot water, as hot as you can stand it, then apply the liniment." He closed his bag and got to his feet. "Stay off it as much as possible for the next few days . . . if you can," he added wryly. "At the very least, take it easy on it."

"Okay, Doc, thanks. What do I owe you?"

"Al will take care of that. Call me if you think you need me."

"Sure."

We both watched him leave, and then I asked Nuss, "Can he keep quiet?"

"No problem," he promised.

"Okay, Al, how much?" I asked.

"Can you pay cash?"

"Yes."

He nodded.

"You done with my services?"

I thought a moment, then said, "I don't think so."

"We'll run a tab," he offered.

It sounded okay to me, and I said so. He told me not to hesitate if I needed anything else. I thanked him and he left.

I soaked my ankle in hot water for a while, and eventually the throbbing decreased to a low roar. I dried it off, wrapped it with gauze I had brought with me, then grabbed my cane and headed for the roof.

The foot felt a little better, but I decided that after my search of the roof I would go right back to my room and stay there the rest of the day. Apparently my cover was blown, and I had to decide how to play it in light of that fact.

On the roof I made a thorough search of the area. I

finally found the spot I wanted. From there I could see Orantes's house very clearly. I was sure that, through a telescopic sight, I'd be able to pick out an ant on the wall. A marksman would have had to be one hell of a shot just to hit the wall from that distance.

I inspected the ledge and found some scratch marks where a rifle could have been mounted for the shot.

The shooter had to be a guest or an employee of the hotel.

Which narrowed it down to just thousands.

I went back to my room, made sure the doors and windows were locked, unwrapped my ankle, and applied the liniment. Then I secured Wilhelmina tightly in my right hand and took a nap.

CHAPTER ELEVEN

I dreamed I was being chased by a group of twenty-year-old assassins, only not only was I being slowed down by a bad foot and a cane, but by old age as well. On top of that, they all looked like Allan Trumball.

The phone woke me up. I looked at the clock and saw that it was nearly 7 P.M. Christine was on the phone, wanting to know if I'd like to join her for dinner. I told her my ankle was bothering me, and that I was going to have something sent up to my room. I told her that if my ankle improved, I might come down for some poker and a nightcap. To her credit, she didn't mention her possibly coming up to the room. She told me she hoped I would feel better and she'd see me later.

I washed my face, then I called room service and asked for some dinner to be sent up, but I specified that Al Nuss bring it.

The phone rang and it was Nuss.

"Nuss here. You need anything besides dinner?"

"No. I'm really hungry, that's all."

"Okay. I'll bring you something special."

"Fine."

About fifteen minutes later he knocked on the door.

"That was quick," I said as he wheeled a tray into the room.

"Well, I'll tell ya," he said, "this was supposed to go to the bridal suite, you know, but I kind of sidetracked it."

He lifted the top of the tray and revealed a dinner fit for a bride and groom.

"Your friends," he added.

"What?"

"The Tremaynes. This was supposed to be theirs."

For some reason I found that particularly funny, and when I stopped laughing I pointed out the fact that there were two settings.

"Staying for dinner?" I asked.

"Are you asking?"

"I'm asking."

"Then I'm staying."

We started to eat, and I realized how truly hungry I was. Getting shot at can sometimes bring that out in you.

"You a cop?" he finally asked.

"No."

"Can't talk, huh?"

"No."

"Okay, no questions," he conceded. "As long as you can pay."

"Cash," I reminded him.

"Right."

Over dessert—we didn't light the candle—he asked. "You need a piece, by any chance?"

"No."

"I can get you a nice one," he pushed.

"Don't necd one," I repeated.

"Okay, okay."

When we finished he covered the tray and headed for the door. I brought out some cash and pushed it into his hand.

"What's this for?"

"Just on account," I told him.

He gave me back the money saying, "Your credit is good, pal. Run the tab, I'll be available."

"Any time?"

"Day or night, twenty-four-hour service."

"I'd rather not have to keep going through the desk," I told him.

He took ot a pen and a pad and wrote down two numbers. One was a hotel number, one was outside.

"What's outside the hotel?" I asked. All I had seen was the big house on the hill.

"I don't like questions either," he said.

I gave him that much.

"Okay, Al. I'll be in touch. Thanks for everything, huh?"

"No problem."

CHAPTER TWELVE

When Nuss left I decided to hit the sack for good. Tomorrow, I told myself, I'd be as good as new, and tomorrow was the day Orantes came to the hotel to gamble. I wanted to be in shape for that.

I opened the bureau in the bedroom and found the note lying on top of the extra packs of gauze I'd brought. It was printed in neat, block letters on hotel stationary.

It read:

> NICK CARTER,
> YOU ARE "THE SPECIALIST'S" 25th
> VICTIM.
> BEWARE!
>
> A FRIEND

I sat down on the bed and read the letter again, with mounting excitement.

The Specialist had been plying his trade successfully for almost four years now, and his trade was killing. Four years, and we had yet to cross paths. In spite of the handicap I was presently laboring under, I was excited at the prospect of finally coming face to face with him.

I was to be victim number twenty-five, which made me next. I had kept up with the Specialist's exploits, and I knew that number twenty-four had been killed with a knife last month in London.

And now it was clearly my turn!

It was now obvious who had taken the shots at me outside of Orantes's place, and it was also clear to me that he had missed on purpose. He was much too good a shot to have missed me twice unless he wanted to.

No one had ever seen the Specialist's face—and lived to tell about it, that is—but perhaps I had and didn't know it. He had to be someone in the hotel, but who? A clerk, a maid, a bellboy?

A bellboy?

Possibly, but I wasn't about to jump to any conclusions. I felt that I had legitimately recognized Al Nuss as being a lot more than he seemed, but that didn't mean that he was the Specialist.

He would definitely be on my list of ten suspects, though.

Just to be sure I didn't jump to any conclusions, I wanted to explore all possibilities.

Number one: The Specialist was here on the island to add me to his list of victims.

Number two: He was here for the auction, recognized me, and decided to add me to his list.

There was something wrong with the second possibility right off. The Specialist never killed for free or for sport; he killed because he was paid to. I was only the backup man on this deal. He'd hit the agent-in-charge first.

Unless he hadn't eyeballed them yet.

I had been in this business a lot longer than they had; my face was not exactly unknown to the opposition. Could be he'd figured me for the agent-in-charge, and decided to send me off the hard way.

No, that didn't scan either.

The Specialist wouldn't be on the island for Orantes's auction, he would be on the island to kill. That was what he did. This meant that, if I was his next victim, some-one must have hired him to kill me, and that someone also had to have known where I would be.

I didn't mind going up against the Specialist. In fact, I relished it, but there were several complications.

First of all, I had a bad ankle and, in spite of it, I had to be on the lookout for the world's number-one-as-sassin.

Next, I had to be there to backup up Casey and Trum-ball, all the while watching my own back. Unfortunate-ly, I had only one set of eyes.

And finally, someone had set me up. Someone knew where I'd be, had passed that information on to the Spe-cialist, and paid him to kill me.

Who knew where I'd be?

David Hawk.

I couldn't afford to start thinking like that. If I trusted no one else in the world, I had to trust Hawk.

Who else knew?

Casey and Trumball? They hadn't seemed to, but I couldn't be that sure.

Hawk had told me that I was requested for this as-signment. Who had requested me? Casey's boss, whoev-er he was.

I could wrack my brain for hours, and there would probably still be someone I didn't know about who knew I'd be here.

And there was yet another question.

Who had written that note? Was it true, or was it just to confuse me, to keep me looking over my shoulder?

Was it the kind of trick—or challenge—the Specialist himself would use?

Game-playing, however, had never been part of the Specialist's reputation.

That brought another thought to mind. His business was hitting what he aimed at, not aiming to miss. If he had done that to me today, it was a first for him.

Casey kept calling this business a game.

It looked like the Specialist might have started thinking the same way.

Maybe it was about time I renamed the game.

CHAPTER THIRTEEN

I removed the false bottom from my suitcase and re-moved my electronics kit which enables me to turn either my radio or television into a communications de-vice.

In this case, I opted for the TV, because I wanted to see Hawk's face when I told him that I was playing tag with the most successful hired killer in the world.

I watched as vertical and horizontal lines dissolved into the face of my boss, David Hawk.

"This does seem to complicate matters," he admitted after I'd given him a rundown of everything that had occurred since my arrival—everything pertinent to the assignment, that is.

He hadn't flinched or blinked when I told him about the note. His face was an impassive mask, which wasn't unusual for him.

"How would you like me to proceed?" I asked.

"Well, knowing you, you don't want to pull out of there," he said. "And knowing you, you wouldn't want me to pull you out either."

"No way. Not when I have a shot—a poor choice of words, I admit—at nailing the number-one assassin of the last decade. Maybe you should bring in another backup for the other two and just let me work on the Specialist," I suggested.

He shook his head gravely.

"The information we are after is very important, Nick. I want you in on this. Perhaps you should let your colleagues in on this, then you can all keep an eye out for the Specialist while working to obtain the information."

"I'll think about it," I told him.

He nodded, saying, "You'll make your own decisions, N3, as always. Whatever you decide to do, do it cautiously, and continue to keep me informed."

"Will do, on both counts."

I broke him up into vertical and horizontal lines again, terminating the contact.

That hadn't helped me all that much. His reaction had been no reaction, and besides, I didn't really suspect David Hawk of anything, did I?

Not really.

But who else knew I'd be on the island?

It was true that Casey and Trumball might not have known who their backup would be, but their superior had to have known.

Should I have asked Hawk who their boss was?

Maybe, but maybe I'd let Casey tell me.

I had decided even before contacting Hawk that I wouldn't clue Casey and Trumball in on the Specialist's presence on the island, since it was obvious that I was his intended victim. They might even be put in less danger not knowing he was around.

Besides, the possibility still existed that perhaps one or both of them already knew he was around.

Casey was the one I'd have to get her boss's name from, because Trumball wouldn't water me if I were a dying geranium.

But that was for tomorrow. Tonight I was going to get

a good night's sleep and hope my foot was much better in the morning. If I was going to face the Specialist, I had to be in the best possible shape.

I stashed the note in my suitcase, undressed and slid under the covers with Wilhelmina, which was something of a comfort. The old girl had never let me down yet.

My ankle continued to throb some, just enough to keep me from falling asleep, which was just as well. When my door opened, ever so softly, I was instantly aware of it. I remained as relaxed and unmoving as possible while sliding my hand under the pillow for Wilhelmina.

I almost overreacted, because I was expecting him, but I was too much of a pro for that. I waited long enough for her perfume to give her away. Then she began making the sounds I've had occasion to become very familiar with: the soft sounds that fabric makes when it rubs against a woman's skin. She was undressing.

The perfume was a dead giveaway. It was a scent that I had never run into again after that first time.

She slid into bed behind me, and I felt the warmth and the smoothness of her flesh against my back. She slid her hands around me and rubbed them up and down my chest and stomach—and then lower. She pressed her hard-tipped breasts against my back, and I began to react.

I turned to face her, and our mouths melted into a long, lingering kiss.

"Nick . . ." she murmured against my mouth.

I silenced her with my mouth as her hands roamed my body. She found Wilhelmina beneath the pillow and took her out.

"We don't need this," she told me, putting it on the night table.

With another kiss the four years melted away, and it

was just as good now as it had been then.

Her body was subtly different, the small differences between a lovely young girl and a beautiful, mature woman. In essence, she was the same; she smelled the same, tasted the same. . . .

. . .and she still said my name, over and over, just before. . . .

CHAPTER FOURTEEN

"Mmm," she moaned afterward, "you've gotten older."

"Thanks a lot."

"And better," she added, smiling slyly, "if that's possible."

She stretched as if she were trying to separate her body into two parts, and while her back was arched and her breasts were pointing their little tips at the ceiling, I playfully tweaked the nipple of the left one.

"Well, you've aged very nicely too," I told her, moving my hand to her right breast and stroking it.

"Really? Like your new girlfriend?"

There was an edge to her voice that I didn't like, and I didn't want to get onto the subject of Christine.

"Do you think this was a wise move?" I asked her.

"Nobody saw me," she assured me, pouting like a little girl. "I've missed you, Nick. You have a way of staying on a girl's mind, you know."

"Flattery won't get you anywhere, Casey. The fact remains that someone could have seen you. Word could get around that the new bride was visiting another man's room in the middle of the night. We don't need that kind of attention."

"Do you really think that's unusual these days?"

"So, maybe I'm old-fashioned."

"Maybe you are," she agreed, running her hand over my chest.

I decided to let that argument go for now.

"Where does Allan think you are right now?" I asked her.

She shrugged.

"I don't know. We don't share a bed, if that's what you're thinking, Nick."

"Now who's being old-fashioned?"

"That's got nothing to do with it. Allan and I are partners, but not in bed—not that he wouldn't like to be. He probably knows where I am right now, or can guess, but I don't really care all that much. It's really none of his business."

She was wrong. As partners in a world where one needs to be able to rely on one's partner, what she did was very much his business—while they were on assignment, that is.

"Won't that make things a little strained?" I asked.

"Between you and him?"

I laughed.

"I don't think things could get much worse between Trumball and me," I told her. "No, I meant between you and him."

She shook her head.

"I can con—I can handle him, Nick, don't worry about that," she assured me. The word she had almost used was *control*, and I was inclined to agree after what I'd seen on the beach.

"Casey, this move of yours was very unprofessional. Not something I would expect of you at all."

"Oh, really?" she asked, rolling over and looping her legs over mine. "I didn't notice you throwing me out of bed. Are you sorry I came?"

Her hands were busy in such a way as to make that

question impossible to answer.

"Besides, I'm entitled to be unprofessional once in four years," she told me, "but it took seeing you again to make it happen."

"I'll take that as a compliment."

"Do."

"Are you still working for the same agency?" I asked.

"Yes. I've had offers from others—including AXE— but I'm satisfied working where I am. I like the policies."

"How's your boss?"

Her eyes narrowed and she asked, "What is this, darling, shop talk?"

"Not exactly," I hedged.

"Then what?"

She sounded curious—or suspicious—which was just what I didn't want. I had to decide how to play it, quickly, and hope that I decided correctly.

I sat up in the bed and rubbed my chin.

"I'm curious, Casey, about why I was sent on this assignment as a backup. You'll admit, I'm not your run-of-the-mill backup agent. Considering my reputation, it's a little more than curious, wouldn't you say?"

"I agree," she answered but offered nothing more.

"Unless I was specifically requested."

"That's possible."

"But who would put in such a request, and why?"

"Well, I might be able to answer the who, but not the why," she offered.

"I'll settle for that—for now."

"It had to be my boss. I don't think your boss would be able to refuse him," she told me, saying "him" as if she were talking about God.

"Why not?"

Her eyes widened and she said, "Well, who could say no to Colonel James J. Lamb?"

"Who indeed?" I echoed.

I knew Lamb, or rather knew of him, by reputation. He was in his mid-fifties, a career army man with a give 'em hell attitude toward politics and everything else. I had heard that he was put in charge of a division of the Secret Service, but exactly which one hadn't been divulged, and at the time I hadn't been all that interested.

But now, I was very interested in Colonel James J. Lamb.

I wondered if he was as interested in me.

"You've heard of him, then?" she asked.

"Oh, yes, I've heard of him, all right. He's kind of hard not to hear of."

"He's a hell-raiser, all right," she agreed, "but he's a good man, Nick. He's no creampuff, and he knows how to get things done, things that no one else has the stomach to do. Some people think his policies and methods are a little harsh, but I think he's simply not afraid to do what has to be done."

"Sounds like you've got a hell of a lot of respect for him," I remarked.

"Oh, I do. I respect him more than any other man I know," she answered. I tried hard not to be hurt.

"Well, why would he want me on this caper as a back-up man?" I asked.

"I don't know, Nick. I don't try to explain what the colonel does; I just do as he says."

"With no questions?"

She nodded her head.

"No questions. Isn't that the way you feel about your boss?" she asked.

I thought of the many arguments I'd had with Hawk over the years and answered, "Not exactly."

Well, at least I knew who her boss was. Now I had to find out if he was the one who had requested my presence on this job and, if so, why.

At the moment, however, Casey's hands were making their presence felt, and becoming very insistent.

I tabled all business for another time.

CHAPTER FIFTEEN

Sometime during the night Casey made an attempt to slip out of my room without waking me, and I let her think she had done so. I wasn't looking forward to running across Trumball the next morning, but he was the least of my worries now. My number-one worry was the Specialist.

Number two, however, was Casey's plan for obtaining this information that Oswaldo Orantes was auctioning off. The problem was, it stunk!

Casey had surprised me twice in the past twenty-four hours. First, with that incredibly bad plan, then with her behavior last night, sneaking into my room. Bad judgment for someone who was supposed to be an experienced professional.

That was just something else that was wrong with this whole assignment.

If the information Orantes had was so important, we were going to need a backup plan for when her plan fell through—and I was damned sure it was going to.

With Casey gone, I fell back to sleep and woke at seven. I grabbed a hot shower, wrapped up my ankle, and got dressed. I had to have breakfast in my room and do just that.

I had to decide just how safe it was for me to go walking around Pleasure Island, and I had to come up with a backup plan for Casey's folly.

I called room service and ordered some eggs and bacon and didn't specify that Al Nuss bring it up. I wanted to see if he would, anyway.

While I waited, I thought about the Specialist. I'd been on the island a couple of days now, and the only attempt on me had been while I was out by Orantes's house, alone. I was pretty sure I would be safe as long as I stayed by the resort, around a lot of people. I had no choice, I had to play it that way.

While showering, I had been touched by the germ of a plan about the information we were ostensibly here to get. The key word that had triggered it had been *gambling*. Casey said that Orantes came to the resort on Saturdays to gamble. If he liked to gamble, I was sure he didn't only do it just on Saturdays, but if he only gambled at the hotel on Saturdays, then where did he gamble on other days?

One of two places. Either off the island—he was wealthy and could go anywhere he wanted—or else, right in his own house.

I intended to be in the hotel casino when Oswaldo Orantes arrived. Meanwhile, I wanted to find out as much about him as I could, and the only person I could think of to help me with that was Al Nuss. I would have to tell him something, however, about why I was interested, something plausible.

When there was a knock at the door I opened it up, and Al Nuss wheeled in a breakfast tray.

I wasn't surprised to see him. This told me that he had to have me under some kind of surveillance—although that might have been kind of a strong word for it.

"You listening in on my calls?" I asked.

He looked at me quickly to see if I was serious, then smiled crookedly. "I am expecting you to be a major source of income to me for the next few days," he told me. "I wanted to make sure you got A-1 service, so I told the desk to give me anything that had to do with your room. Do you mind?"

I shook my head.

"No, I don't. In fact, I wanted to talk to you today about something. Did you bring an extra cup?"

He lifted the tray cover, revealing not only an extra cup, but an extra place setting as well.

"Are we going to be meal companions from now on, too?" I asked.

"Only when I'm invited, and I like to be prepared. C'mon, it's gonna get cold," he warned, pulling up a chair.

In spite of myself, I was looking at Al Nuss through different eyes. I could very well have been sitting there having breakfast with the Specialist. The food could have been poisoned—but then again, that wasn't the Specialist's style. He was more direct and went right to his victim, which also made yesterday's incident that much more puzzling.

I was too much of a pro to let the Specialist's presence on the island immobilize me completely. I was just going to have to operate normally, and wait for him to come for me—and be ready.

So for now, Al Nuss was Al Nuss, and nothing more.

"So what did you want me for?" he asked around a mouthful of eggs that I was paying for.

"Look, Al, I'm going to level with you," I told him.

"Oh, you mean you haven't been?" he asked with mock surprise.

"No, I haven't been," I repeated, "and we both know it. My name is Nick Collins, but I'm not a college professor. I'm a private investigator, working out of Washington, D.C."

"Private Dick, huh? I figured you had to be something like that. What's the case you're on?"

"I can't give you all of the details, but it involves the big house on the other side of the island."

"Orantes's house. You plan on getting involved with Oswaldo Orantes?"

"It looks like it. I need to know something about him, Al, and I think you're probably the one to fill me in. Am I right?"

He thought about it.

"If you're gonna play with Orantes, you're playing in the big leagues, Nick. I guess I can fill you in on what I know—it'll give you a better chance."

We were down to just coffee and I poured us each a cup.

"You talk, I'll listen," I told him.

"Okay. Orantes started this Pleasure Island business. Some say he bought the island with mob money. The mob backed him, they said, but they didn't have a piece of the action. You and I know that doesn't sound like the mob, but supposedly, Orantes paid it all back and it's his free and clear.

"I've also heard that Orantes is in the buying and selling business. He buys whatever there is to be bought, and sells it to whoever comes up with the most money." His eyes narrowed at this point and he said, "You're working out of Washington, D.C., right? Has this got something to do with the feds? Are the feds after Orantes?"

"Al, you're supposed to be doing the talking, remember?"

He held up both hands and said, "Okay, sorry. Let's see . . . buying and selling, right?"

"Right. Listen, has he got anything to sell right now?"

He thought a moment, then nodded, saying, "Word has it."

"Any idea what it is?"

He nodded. "None at all."

"Okay, tell me more. What is he like?"

"Like? Like any wealthy man, full of himself—thinks he's a king because he's The Man on Pleasure Island. He struts into the casino every Saturday night and plops down at the poker table and cleans everyone out."

"Wait a minute. The poker table? He plays poker?"

"Does a fish swim?"

"Nothing else?"

"Never. Just poker."

"Once a week? That doesn't sound right."

"It's not. I've heard that he has a game at his house three times a week, then comes here on Saturdays."

"Does he eat dinner here on Saturday?"

"Yes, and he usually picks up some pretty little plaything to share it with."

"What kind of women does he like?"

"Married blondes, young ones."

Well, Casey had that right, at least.

"How does he work his Saturdays?"

"How do you mean?"

"Does he eat and then gamble, or gamble and then eat?"

"Uh, he has dinner, then he hits the table."

"When does he pick up the girl?"

"Before dinner."

"What does he do with the husband?"

He shrugged.

"They always seem to find something else to do," he said.

"Do they ever disappear?"

"You mean, permanently?"

I nodded.

"No. Sometimes the husband and wife leave the island separately, but they both always leave."

"What does Orantes look like?"

"He's in his forties, heavyset, short white hair, pouchy eyes."

"Bodyguards?"

"Sure, two, at all times."

I thought it all over, then asked, "Okay, Al, now tell me, how do I impress Mr. Orantes?"

"That's easy," he told me. "Beat him at poker."

CHAPTER SIXTEEN

Al left with the tray after once again asking me if I needed a piece.

"I've got one," I told him.

"I can get you a nice—"

"I've got what I need, Al, thanks. Thanks for the information, too."

"Sure, it all goes on the bill."

"Right."

"Listen, if you're gonna deal with Orantes, be careful, huh? He ain't no Washington politician's runaway daughter, you know."

I nodded. "Sure, thanks."

He nodded, wheeled the tray out, and shut the door behind him. Almost as soon as he left, the phone rang.

"Good morning, Nick."

It was Christine.

"How are you feeling?"

"Much better, thanks."

"Do you think a swim might help your ankle?" she asked.

"I don't see how it could hurt," I told her. "I'll meet you on the beach in fifteen minutes."

"Fine. I'll be the girl who's almost in her bathing suit."

"I can't wait."

I hung up, thinking it was too bad that Christine wasn't a blonde. That plus her poker abilities would almost make her a sure bet for attracting Orantes.

Maybe he'd make an exception in her case.

I changed into a bathing suit and terry cloth robe and decided to leave my cane behind. I unwrapped my ankle, and it felt pretty good. I made my way down to the beach very slowly, so I wouldn't aggravate the injury.

I spotted her right away. All I had to do was follow the direction of all the male heads. They were all turned toward her.

She was wearing a one-piece bathing suit that was the same color as her tan. It seemed as if she had nothing on, which I suppose is what she had meant on the phone. She had large, very round breasts and full thighs, which other women would consider too heavy but men would love. I waved and she waved back, and everyone looked at me.

The Specialist could have been out there on that beach looking at me with all of the other tourists. My back started to itch, but I ignored it and approached Christine.

"You look fabulous," I told her.

"You don't look too bad yourself. Let's swim out to the float," she suggested, pointing out to the sea. The float was far enough out so that you had to be a pretty good swimmer to even consider it.

"Race?" I asked.

"I wouldn't presume to take advantage of an injured man. Why don't we just go at a nice, leisurely pace, hmm?"

"You're on."

I dropped my robe, and we walked into the water hand-in-hand.

She was a marvelous swimmer, cutting through the

water with smooth, powerful strokes. I'm a very strong swimmer, and she didn't lag behind me an inch. When we reached the float I hoisted myself up on it and helped her up beside me. Her suit was plastered to her body, and her nipples were distended from the cool water.

"Jesus Christ," I said.

"Pardon?" she answered, pushing her hair back and giving me a coy look.

"I'm about to commit a crime right here in plain sight," I told her.

"Should I stay and be a witness?" she asked.

I was about to explain that she was to be the victim when something whizzed by my ear and buried itself in the float right behind me.

"Get off!" I shouted, pushing Christine off the float, back into the water.

"Hey!" she shouted.

There was another whiz-bang before I followed her into the water.

"Behind the float," I told her.

"What's going on?" she demanded. "Is this a joke?"

"It's no joke, Christine," I told her once I got her behind the float. "Someone is shooting at us."

"At us?"

"Probably at me."

"Are you kidding?"

"Do I look like I'm kidding?" I asked.

I inched up to look over the float, trying to inspect the beach and the hotel. From the roof, this float would look like a postage stamp. I couldn't see if there was anyone up there with a rifle or anything else, but I knew he had been there. It would take a shot like the Specialist to hit a postage stamp-sized target at that distance.

Two shots, just like the last time.

Two deliberate misses, also. Of that I was sure.

Well, at the very least, the incident had enabled me to

scratch one person off my list. Christine had been right beside me when the shots were fired.

"Nick."

"Yeah?"

"Is he gone?"

"I can't tell, but I think so. I can't see where the shots came from, but I'm sure it was the roof."

"Can we go back in?" She sounded scared.

I looked at her and smiled, trying to put her at ease.

"Sure, but let's swim in as far as we can underwater, okay? Just to be on the safe side."

"Okay, but once we get back, you owe me an explanation, okay?"

Since, theoretically, she had been in as much danger as I had, I agreed to do so.

"You're on. C'mon, I'll race you back. Loser buys dinner."

I gave her a short kiss, then ducked my head under and took off for shore. I could feel her presence at my side the whole way. I shortened my stride just a bit when I felt my feet touch bottom, so that I'd have to pay for dinner. I owed her at least that much for the scare she'd just had.

When we came out of the water it seemed much too quiet, as if everyone was watching us. I was sure that no one was aware of what had happened. We were too far out for that. The unnatural quiet was just a direct result of the incident. After a moment the regular beach noises began to filter through the roaring in my ears as I pounded the water out of them.

"You owe me dinner," Christine said, out of breath.

"It'll be my pleasure."

"And an explanation, don't forget," she reminded me.

"Let's get dried off," I told her. "Then we'll go on the veranda for a drink and I'll explain."

I had decided to give her the same story I had given Al Nuss, about being a private detective. I hoped that she would believe it, the way he apparently had.

I asked her if she wanted to change, but she said she'd rather stay the way she was. I put on my robe and we went to the veranda bar.

Once we were settled with our drinks, I told her essentially the same story I told Al, about being involved with a case that concerned Oswaldo Orantes.

"The man in the big house?" she asked.

"You know about him?" I said.

"Uh, yes, as a matter of fact, I do know something about him," she answered. I had a feeling she was holding back, but I wanted to finish my story.

"Well, I've got to get in to see him, Christine, and I understand that he's a poker player—not a gambler, but strictly a poker player. He comes here to play on Saturday nights."

"I know that, Nick. That's why I'm here," she confessed.

"Ah-ha, I see. Does it also have something to do with his private games?"

"It has everything to do with them. I was hoping to play against him this evening and impress him enough to get invited to his private sessions."

I nodded. That was exactly my plan, also. I knew that would be what I would have to do as soon as Al had mentioned that the only way to impress him was to beat him at poker.

"Looks like we're both thinking along the same lines," I told her.

"Which means we'll be playing against each other this evening," she observed. "Not with the same results, I hope," she added.

Damn! This was a complication I didn't need.

"Christine, it's very important that I play in that game tonight—"

"Nick, please," she interrupted. "Don't ask me not to play. It's the only reason I'm here."

It wouldn't be fair to her to ask her not to play; I knew that.

The simple truth of the matter was, I was afraid of her. I was afraid that her beauty coupled with her playing ability would eclipse my chance of impressing Orantes enough to get an invitation to play at his home.

"I won't ask you not to play, Christine. I realize that it's important to you."

She leaned across the table and asked, "Is this supposed to be reverse psychology?"

I put my elbow on the table and my chin in my hand and answered, "It was sort of a lame attempt, yeah."

"Nick, I'm sorry we have to play against each other, but I always play to win."

"So do I, I'm afraid."

"Well, maybe we'll bring the best out in each other," she proposed.

"Let's talk about it again at dinner tonight," I offered.

"Okay, but you can't talk me out of playing," she warned.

I rose and said, "I realize that, Christine. Why don't I call your room about six, and we'll make plans for when we're going to eat, okay?"

"Okay."

I started to walk away and she called, "Nick?"

"Yeah," I said, turning.

"I'm not going to get shot at again, am I?"

I shook my head.

"*I* got shot at, Christine. You just happened to be there with me."

"You never told me who you think shot at you," she pointed out.

"I haven't the faintest idea," I lied.

"Well, do me a favor, huh? Try not to get shot between now and dinner?"

"I'll do my best," I promised.

On the way back to my room I stopped at the desk and left a message for Al Nuss to call me at his earliest convenience. When I was opening my door a couple of seconds later, the phone was already ringing.

"Yeah?"

"Al Nuss," he said.

"Yeah, Al, I've got one more question I forgot to ask you."

"Shoot."

"What time does Orantes usually stop into the hotel for dinner on Saturdays?"

He answered without hesitation.

"There's no 'usually' about it. He comes for dinner at exactly eight, finishes at exactly nine, and then hits the tables."

"You've got it pinpointed that precisely?"

"Listen, the big man's comings and goings are not exactly unnoticeable," he pointed out.

"I guess not," I agreed. "Thanks, Al."

"Hey, Nick?"

"What?"

"When do I get let in on the whole story, huh?"

"Soon, Al, very soon. Thanks again."

"Sure."

I hung up and checked my watch. I decided to give Christine a few more minutes to get back to her room before calling.

I wanted to be in the dining room when Orantes arrived, and I also wanted to be at the poker table before he sat down. I was sure Christine would want the same.

I called after I'd showered and dressed, rewrapping my ankle with care. It felt pretty good, no ill effects from the swimming. That pleased me more than anything else.

When she answered I said, "Hi, it's Nick."

"Impatient," she scolded.

"No, I just thought you'd want to know early. Orantes sits down to dinner at eight."

"I could have told you that."

I stared at the phone, then wondered why I was surprised. She had obviously done her homework.

"Well then, I'll pick you up at your room at seven thirty. Let's make sure we're already there when he gets there, okay?"

"I'm for that. See you then."

"Okay. Dress for poker, huh?"

"Baby, I'll be dressed to kill," she promised.

That was what I was afraid of.

CHAPTER SEVENTEEN

The Specialist was still playing games with me. He was trying for a psychological edge, which meant he was either afraid of me or he respected me a great deal. I chose to believe the latter. I didn't think the Specialist was afraid of anyone, but he was being a little overly cautious with me. I hoped to be able to use that to my advantage.

Almost immediately after I hung up, the phone rang again. The ringing sounded unusually harsh, like an angry scream.

I answered by simply saying, "Yes?"

"Where have you been?" a man's voice demanded angrily.

It was Trumball.

"Out for a swim," I told him.

"You're supposed to be available to me at all times," he told me. Not "us," but "me." He was still playing the boss.

"Tremayne, what do you want?" I asked.

He bit back a retort and hesitated, as if attempting to compose himself. God help me if he wasn't actually trying to be professional. Too little, too late, pal.

"Mrs. Tremayne and I would like you to join us for

lunch on the veranda, Mr. Collins," he said politely through tightly clenched teeth. I wondered if Casey was there with him, forcing him to make the call and extend the invitation.

"Why, that sounds lovely, Mr. Tremayne. What time shall I meet you and the missus?"

"Twelve," he answered shortly.

"I'll be there. Thank your wife for me, won't you? I'm sure it was her idea."

He was about to say something else but thought better of it and hung up abruptly.

Just what I needed, lunch on the veranda with Trumball. At least Casey would be there to run interference.

Once again I considered telling both of them about the two shooting incidents, and once again I rejected the idea out of pure instinct.

I sat on the bed, resting my ankle until lunch. I used the time to clean Wilhelmina. I wanted her to be ready for the big day, the showdown with the Specialist, whenever it came.

I went over what I knew about the world's greatest assassin since he'd first come on the scene four years ago.

In the beginning they didn't know what to call him. Some people in the business called him the Challenger, because he seemed to challenge his victims to their specialties, then beat them at it.

Victim number five was a marksman, and he was killed from a single bullet fired at a range of over two hundred yards.

Victim number fourteen was an expert at the martial arts, and he was killed without a weapon. His neck was broken.

It was about this time that they started calling the killer the Specialist. All of his victims were agents—of all countries—and all were killed by their own specialty.

Victim number twenty-four had been killed just under a month ago.

He had been an acquaintance of mine, a man I had worked with on occasion and respected. He had also been an expert with any kind of a blade. He had been killed with a knife while holding his own knife in his hand. Apparently, it had been a fair fight, each having an equal opportunity to kill the other—only agent Bob Lace had not been equal to the task.

It's very possible that the Specialist may have been credited with a few deaths that weren't his work, but my own count was twenty-four, and I felt that I was pretty adept at recognizing one of his jobs. The note I'd received had pretty much justified that much.

I was to be victim number twenty-five. And since the Specialist's m.o. was killing agents by the use of their own specialties, we were in a little trouble.

You see, I don't have a specialty.

That is to say, I do everything with equal efficiency and expertise. I can shoot and I can handle a knife. If Wilhelmina and Hugo could talk, they'd testify to that. As far as martial arts, I don't lay any claim to a particular color belt, but I can handle myself in close quarters.

The Specialist had his pick, and I had to be ready for any of them, so before joining my colleagues for lunch, I thoroughly cleaned Wilhelmina and gave Hugo a few practice tosses. Pierre, taped to my thigh, was a possible ace in the hole.

Then I went to lunch.

"Good afternoon, Nick," Casey greeted.

"Good afternoon," I said, sitting across from Trumball. That put Casey on my left, and the beach on my right.

"Are we on first name basis now?" I asked.

Trumball started to answer, but Casey cut him off with a wave of her hand.

"I think Mr. Collins and the Tremaynes can assume a first name basis at this point in their relationship without arousing anyone's suspicion, don't you, Nick?"

"I certainly do, Casey," I agreed, resisting the urge to lean over and whisper, loud enough for Trumball to hear, "especially you and I."

"Good. What we want to discuss, Nick, is your placement during our operation tonight."

"I'm having dinner with a friend tonight," I told her. She knew who the friend was, and she didn't like it. I saw the muscles in her jaw twitch.

"I think that as backup agent—" she began.

"As backup agent," I interrupted, "I should be in the vicinity when you launch your vamp act at Oswaldo Orantes in the casino tonight—or will that be at eight, when he comes for dinner?" I asked.

"How did you know—" Trumball began, but Casey shut him up again.

"You've done your homework, Nick," Casey observed.

"I don't like being in the dark, Casey, and that's where I've been on this assignment. I'm going to have dinner with a friend tonight, then I plan on doing a little gambling—as a cover, naturally. I'll be around to back you up," I told her, then I couldn't resist adding, "You need all the help you can get," indicating Trumball.

"Dammit, Car—Col—" Trumball was so mad he didn't know what to call me.

I grabbed a menu from the table and asked them both, "Shall we order lunch?"

CHAPTER EIGHTEEN

When Christine opened the door in answer to my knock she pulled me inside and shut the door quickly, then started patting me down, as if she were searching for something.

"What are you looking for?" I asked.

She continued to pat as she answered, "Holes." She patted some more, then stepped back and said, "No, I don't see any."

"There aren't any," I assured her.

Then I took a good look at her.

She was dressed to kill, all right. Her outfit was a tight-fitting jumpsuit that went to her neck but had no shoulders or sleeves. It accentuated the deep thrust of her breasts, and she wore no bra underneath. It was almost more revealing than if she had worn something scoop-necked to show a lot of flesh. Also, there were panels cut out on either side the outfit, showing off the well-tanned and firm flesh of her waist.

"Beautiful," was all I could say.

"Thank you. Shall we go? We want to get there before Orantes does."

"Yes, we do. Let's go."

By seven fifty we were seated at a table in the dining room, walking right past a line of people to get it. I had made arrangements through Al Nuss for the table and only had to slip the maitre d' a ten in addition.

"Nice table," Christine commented. "We can see the whole dining room."

"That's the idea," I told her.

"Is this what private eyes do?" she asked.

"What?"

"Sit around in expensive restaurants, entertaining expensive ladies . . ."

"Are you expensive?"

Nodding, she continued, " . . . watching for rich, powerful men?"

"Only when I've got a reasonably wealthy client who can foot the bills."

"How often is that?"

"Not very often. Most of the work is very dull, very routine. It isn't often I get to come to a place like this, mingle with monied people. I'm not used to it."

"That's funny."

"What?"

"Well, you act as if you're used to it. You dress well, you know what wines to order—"

Too many questions.

"Research, my dear. I do my homework," I told her, repeating the phrase Casey had used that afternoon.

"And very well, too. Very well."

I didn't think she was swallowing my whole line, but I was spared any further questions by the arrival of the man we were waiting for, the man we both wanted to impress for different reasons.

He himself was impressive.

He generated activity, a flurry of it. Waiters flocked to him, making obvious the fact that, not only was he the boss, he was probably a big tipper as well.

"Your table is ready, Mr. Orantes," the maitre d' told him. Behind him, to his left and right, stood his two bodyguards. They were well dressed, big but not muscle-bound, and they divided the room into two equal parts and surveyed only their half.

Orantes surprised me.

I expected a Hispanic-looking gentleman, but Orantes's dark skin was from the sun, not heredity. His hair, cut in almost a crewcut, was snow white. He was massive, not fat, but incredibly big, and it was all in the upper half of his body.

The maitre d' led the way to his table. One of the bodyguards descended the steps ahead of the big man, one behind him, and a waiter followed him. They marched single file to a large table in a corner of the room.

"That's him," Christine announced.

"I guessed."

"I didn't have to," she told me.

"What? You knew what he looked like?"

"Well, I saw him, once. He's a legend in poker, you know," she explained. "My father played him years ago."

"How did he do?"

"He got cleaned out."

"That's comforting. A legend, huh?"

"Yep."

I watched the legend as he ordered dinner for himself and his two bodyguards. They didn't speak, so it was obvious that they ate whatever their boss ordered for them, drank whatever he drank.

"There's your friend," Christine said suddenly.

"Where?" I asked, looking at her even though I knew who she meant.

"The new bride," she answered, nodding her head toward the entrance.

Casey and Trumball were just entering the dining room. Casey had chosen the alternate route from the one Christine had picked. She was showing skin, and a lot of it. She wore a low-cut gown that plunged deep between her breasts, and even further in the back. She had piled what was left of her once long hair atop her head. Trumball walked along behind her, looking over the room. When he spotted Orantes—recognizing him either from his description or from a photo—he said something to her. She did not look over at the big man, but if she had she would have been in for a big surprise.

He wasn't looking at her, either.

CHAPTER NINETEEN

I watched Orantes all through dinner, and in spite of the fact that Casey and Trumball must have paid a bundle to get a table near him, I never saw him look at Casey once. By the same token, I never saw him look at any woman, Casey, Christine, anyone. He seemed totally engrossed in his dinner.

So I started watching his bodyguards, first one, then the other. Maybe they were his blonde-spotters, but their eyes moved continuously around the room, never stopping and resting on any one person for very long.

"He can pack it away, can't he?" Christine commented.

"He sure can." Indeed, he was totally devoted, it seemed, to consuming as much food as he could in the one hour he allotted himself for dinner. The bodyguards ate sparingly, so as not to detract from their continuous crowd inspection.

Casey seemed to be getting slightly edgy. I could tell because she kept sneaking glances at the big man from time to time, then her eyes would slide from him to me and away again. Trumball was just outright nervous. He kept chain-smoking and draining his water glass. With the number of times he had called for a waiter to fill his glass, he was starting to attract attention.

"I think we'd better hit the table" I told Christine. "It's eight fifty." I called for the check and signed it, fulfilling our bet of that afternoon.

When we got to the poker table—the high stakes game, of course—there was only one seat available.

"The lady?" the dealer asked. Forced into playing the gentleman, I allowed Christine to take the seat. Looking the table over, I saw that there were at least two who were playing over their heads. They were the small-timers and tourists who had wanted just one try at the big table, and they were just about tapped out.

Of course, I was just about in the same predicament as they were: lack of funds. I hadn't intended on playing any high stakes poker during this assignment, so my finances were not in a position to withstand a streak of bad luck. I wondered idly if Al Nuss would be in a position to extend a sizable loan along with all of his other capabilities. Of course, if things became really tight, I could always wire Hawk for some additional funds. Right now I was about five minutes away from sitting down with Pleasure Island's version of The Man, so the cash I had on me would have to do.

"Sir?" the dealer said.

"Pardon?"

"I was saying, there's an empty seat now, sir," he repeated patiently.

I saw one of the tourists getting up from the table, shaking his head sadly.

"Oh, sorry," I told the dealer. "Thank you."

I sat down and barely had time to buy some chips when Orantes made his entrance.

"Good evening, Mr. Orantes," the dealer greeted him as he approached the table.

"James, good evening," the big man said in return. "Have you a seat for me?"

"Of course, sir. Right here."

I hadn't noticed, but now I could see that the dealer had indeed been saving a seat for Orantes. The big man made himself as comfortable as the chair would allow, purchased some chips—about three times the amount I had bought—and began inspecting the players at the table. One bodyguard stood right behind him, the other seemed to be strolling aimlessly about, but I could see that he was watching and waiting.

Okay, so now I was sitting at the poker table with Orantes. There were seven players and once again, as if by design, I had drawn the chair directly opposite Christine. She smiled at me and I smiled back. Friendly rivals wishing each other good luck.

Orantes was two players to my left. If Christine was seated at twelve o'clock and I was at six o'clock, he was at nine o'clock.

"Would anyone object to limiting the play to five card stud?" Orantes asked the dealer, loud enough for the entire table to hear.

"Certainly not, Mr. Orantes," the dealer assured him. There was a general nodding of heads around the table. All but one of the players seemed to be serious poker players who realized who Orantes was. The last of the small-timers would be gone soon.

"Shall we get on with the game, then?" Orantes asked.

"Certainly, sir."

The first hand began. Each player was in turn, theoretically, the dealer, although the house always dealt. The play would start to the left of the theoretical dealer, which, with this hand, just happened to be me.

I watched as the cards were dealt. A king fell to Orantes—coincidence, right?—and a ten to Christine. When the last card fell—mine—it was the ace, leaving the matter of opening the betting to me. I opened with the minimum. The two players between Orantes and me called, and Orantes raised the same amount. Everyone else, including Christine, called my bet and his raise. I called his raise, and the two players between him and me both dropped out.

I had a queen in the hole, but the next time around Orantes drew another king. He bet double the minimum on his pair; everyone stayed until it got to me. I folded and was content to watch the hand develop.

I was watching Orantes and he was watching Christine. Of the players left in the hand, he had already tabbed her as the one to beat. She was showing a pair of tens.

By the time all of the face-up cards were dealt, the player to my right had developed two pair, albeit low ones, deuces and threes. He made his bet but did it tentatively, indicating he had nothing better. All the players between he and Orantes were gone, so Orantes immediately raised. I figured him for at least three kings. The player between the big man and Christine folded, and Christine, still showing tens, reraised. I figured her for at least three tens, until she raised. She must have had tens full, unless she was trying to force the two pair out, affording her a better chance of filling her hand. The two pair, however, called both raises, and Orantes called Christine's.

The final card was dealt, and the leader on board, the two pair, passed. He hadn't improved. Orantes, however, bet into Christine, in spite of the fact that she had raised him previously. Christine wasted no time in raising him, and the player to my right, realizing that he had stayed too long at the fair, immediately dropped out.

Orantes regarded Christine closely, her eyes and her cards, and then called her raise.

She turned her cards over, and the dealer called her hand.

"Four tens."

Without expression, Orantes threw his cards in, face

down. He had bet into her, despite her raise, which meant he had to have had kings full. He had figured her for tens full, but luck had been with her. I was willing to bet that her seventh card had been the fourth ten.

"Four tens, the winner," the dealer called. "New hand begins."

Round one to Christine, I thought.

For the next hour, two players won consistently: Orantes and Christine. I had fallen into the situation I had been hoping against: a run of bad luck. I had been getting decent hands, but continued to come out second best.

I had actually been able to last out the hour by bluffing on two hands successfully, both of which had not included either Orantes or Christine. Neither one of them would have let my bluff go by in either case. At the end of the hour, my poke was down to half what it had been, and the only thing to do was take a break and hope my luck would change when I returned.

"I'll be back in a few moments," I told the dealer.

"You'll have to surrender the seat, sir, if someone else wishes to play," the dealer informed me regretfully.

"James," Orantes spoke up before I could object.

"Yes, sir?"

"Hold the seat for the gentleman. He has too much invested up to this point."

"Of course, sir. All right, Mr. Collins," James told me, obviously remembering me from the other night, "we will hold your seat."

"Thank you, James." I turned to Orantes and added, "And thank you, sir."

He didn't look at me but raised his hand as if to say, don't mention it.

Christine gave me a pitying smile and a shake of her head. I smiled back with false bravado and went for a drink.

At the bar I ordered a bourbon and was half through with it when I felt a tap on my shoulder. I turned to find a waiter handing me an envelope.

"A message, sir."

I looked at him curiously, took the message, and said, "Thank you."

I set my glass down and opened the envelope to read the message. In the envelope was enough cash to keep me in the game even if I lost steadily for the next two hours. There was a small piece of napkin upon which was written: GO GET HIM. The note was unsigned.

Someone watching the game—or in it—had realized that, the way my luck was running, I would soon be tapped out. Who else could it be but Christine?

Against my better judgement, I decided to accept the cash and use it, but I'd speak to her about it afterward.

Now all I had to hope for was a change of luck.

I did, however, have one source of solace, and that was Orantes himself. He had instructed the dealer to hold my seat. There could have been many reasons for that, but perhaps he saw something in my play that he liked. I had been playing well, and getting decent hands, but you never won with second best. Not at anything, least of all cards.

I went back to the table and reclaimed my seat. There were only six of us now, the last small-timer having dropped out in my absence. He had done well to last that long. There was now one player between myself and Orantes.

"New hand, sir," James informed me. I nodded my thanks, and he dealt me in.

With the extra money in my pocket I felt much more relaxed and confident. It also seemed to affect my luck. James the dealer gave me aces, back to back. In five card stud, that's almost an unbeatable start.

I opened for a hundred dollars, twice the amount of

any of my previous bets. Orantes looked at me, which was the only outward indication that he was puzzled. There was no expression on his face; but he had looked straight at me for the first time.

He was wondering why I changed my tactics.

Showing a king, he raised me immediately. It was odd, the amount of times he had gotten kings that night. Christine, with a seven of clubs showing, called my bet and also called his raise. All of the others stayed in until I reraised. After that it was just the three of us.

James dealt the third card of the hand.

I received a six of hearts, Orantes a three to go with his king. Christine got a six of spades to go with the seven of clubs.

The betting went the same way. I bet, Orantes raised, Christine called, I reraised, he called, and so did she.

The dealer gave us our fourth card.

To go with my ace and six, I got a seven. All were different suits. I bet a hundred again.

Orantes got a five to go with his king and three. Again, mismatched suits, but he raised. He had to have another king in the hole. He was playing strong, hoping that, even if I had aces, he'd buy. The problem was, if we both bought, he lost anyway.

And then there was Christine.

Sitting with a mismatched six and seven, she bought an eight. She had a straight in the making, and she surprised both of us by raising Orantes. The most she could have had was a pair of eights, so she was playing for the straight. I called both of their raises, and Orantes called hers. We both knew we had her beat, unless she bought. She must have been sitting with a five or a nine in the hole. She wouldn't raise unless she was open at both ends. For example, if she had a ten in the hole, the only card that could help her would be a nine. She wouldn't play for one card. If she had a five in the hole, she needed a four or a nine, and if she had the nine, she needed a five or a ten. With her luck running good, she was going for it.

Now we awaited our last card, all looking to buy something.

I bought an eight of diamonds, which was no help at all. With all of my cards before me, I still had aces—and that was it.

Orantes bought another king, giving him two on board, and a possible third in the hole. His face revealed nothing.

Christine got a ten. If she had a nine in the hole, she was unbeatable.

I bet like I had something, two hundred dollars.

Orantes looked at me, then at my cards. He had to figure I had the aces—either that, or I was an idiot. This was his dilemma. If all he had was kings, he could raise me, trying to steal the hand. Then again, if he had a king in the hole, giving him trips, or if he had a card in the hole matching one of the others on the table, giving him two pair, he'd definitely raise, knowing full well he beat my aces.

He had no choice but to raise.

"Make it four hundred," he said quietly, throwing the chips in.

Christine was in the same boat. If she had the nine, she couldn't lose. If she raised, chances were good she had it, but if she didn't and one of us stayed in to see her, she was dead.

She played it like she had it, saying, "Make it eight."

One or two—hell—or *all* of us, were lying. So far I knew I wasn't but they didn't. I knew that what I had, beat what they had . . . showing.

"I call."

Orantes looked at Christine now. If he bought, he only had her to worry about, because he knew he beat me. If he didn't buy, he knew I had him beat, and he'd go out. If he called, I knew I was dead, and it would be up to Christine to beat him.

"I call," he said.

I was dead.

If he had folded, I would have had a good shot, because I didn't think Christine had the straight.

We both watched as she turned over her hole card: a three of spades. She had bluffed, and lost.

Now it was my turn. I turned over my hole card, revealing the fact that I had aces, the same pair I'd had from the beginning, and had been unable to improve on.

Orantes flipped his card: a five of clubs, matching the five he had showing.

"Kings over fives," James called, "the winner."

He'd beaten me with his last card. I shrugged and waited for the next deal.

During the next hour, I won more than I lost. I still hadn't had to touch the extra money in my pocket, but the fact that it was there had changed my play. At that point, Orantes, Christine, and I seemed to be on an even par.

"James," Orantes said, and the dealer leaned over so the big man could whisper in his ear. He nodded and then stood up.

"The table limit has been doubled," he announced. Obviously, Orantes had dictated some new rules to him, wanting to separate the men from the boys. "When a chair empties, it will stay empty until the end of the game."

We all nodded, and in another hour the game was down to just three players: Oswaldo Orantes, Christine Hall, and myself. I had really gotten involved in the game and was enjoying myself immensely.

"Final hand," James suddenly announced, "limit is lifted completely."

This had to have been done on a prearranged signal from Orantes.

I checked my watch and found that it was almost one. We'd been playing for four hours, and a crowd had gathered around the table to watch. When James made his announcement, they started to buzz.

"Quiet, please," the dealer announced.

I made a quick check of the crowd but saw neither Casey nor Trumball.

I settled myself in my chair and waited for the first card. It all came down to this hand.

James dealt.

I received a king of diamonds, Orantes got a queen of hearts, and Christine a nine of diamonds.

I did not look at my hole card, and bet five hundred. It didn't matter what I had in the hole, I had to be in on this hand.

Without hesitation, Orantes raised five hundred. Christine called, and so did I.

Next card.

Me: a ten of diamonds, to go with the king.

Orantes: an ace of clubs for his queen of hearts.

Christine paired her nines, making her boss on board.

She bet five hundred. I called. Orantes hesitated a moment, then raised with a what-the-hell motion. Christine called. If he paired either one of his table cards, he had her beat. She was content to wait a while and see what developed. I called again.

James dealt us our fourth card.

Me: a deuce of hearts, no help.

Orantes: a jack of spades, to go with his ace and queen. A possible straight, while the probabilities were better for either aces or queens, since his raise had been done before the jack.

Christine received an eight of clubs, which was no apparent help. However, since she bet five hundred, despite Orantes's previous raise, I figured her for another eight in the hole, giving her two pair.

Feeling trapped, I called the bet.

Orantes caught and held her eyes for about ten full seconds, then raised a thousand dollars. He was raising on possibilities: he was either waiting for a card for the high straight, or he had a pair and was hoping for two pair, or three of a kind, either of which would beat her two pair.

Christine had no choice. She couldn't fold two pair. She had a shot at a full house, which would even negate his straight.

She raised a thousand.

If this had just been another poker game, I would have been long gone, but I said a little prayer and threw two thousand dollars' worth of chips into the pot.

For the first time, I saw something in Orantes's face. He knew why Christine was in the hand, but what the hell was I doing?

He called her raise, and James gave us our last card.

Me: a ten of clubs, giving me a pair of tens showing.

Orantes: an ace, giving him a pair of aces.

Christine: An ace of hearts, no apparent help.

The play was to Orantes, with his aces.

He had to play it strong, and he did.

"Twenty-five hundred," he called, shoveling it in.

Christine took it well, without expression. She did check her hole card, but then she called—and raised a thousand.

Thirty-five hundred to me, and I hadn't even checked my hole card.

I took the extra money from my pocket, counted out thirty-five hundred, and threw the cash in with the chips.

"I call."

Orantes threw in Christine's thousand and raised another fifteen hundred. She called, and I got pissed. I admit, I just wanted to shake the big man up. I was caught up in the current of the whole game. I counted what I had left in the envelope: sixty-five hundred.

That's what I raised.

All or nothing.

That got his attention.

He had me beat if all we both had was what was showing. If he didn't call, if he went out, and then Christine did, too, he wouldn't have been able to sleep for weeks.

He called, his hand shaking ever so slightly. It wasn't the money, just the tension of the game, the excitement.

I felt it myself.

Christine knew she had us both if all we had was what was showing, so she had no choice but to call.

As if we had timed it beforehand, we all turned our cards over at the same time.

Orantes's card was a five of diamonds. All he had were the aces on board.

Christine turned over an eight, giving her two pair, nines and eights.

I saw my hole card at the same time everyone else did: a deuce of diamonds.

"Tens over deuces," James called my hand, "the winner."

The crowd oohed, Christine nodded to me, and Orantes stood up. The bodyguards immediately took up their positions, one to the right, one to the left, one pace back.

"Thank you, Mr. Collins, and Miss—"

"Hall," she told him, "Christine Hall."

"Miss Hall. Thank you both for a very interesting game. James," he said, handing the dealer a hundred dollar bill, "have my chips cashed and the money delivered to my home. Thank you."

"Certainly, sir. Good night."

Orantes left, bodyguards trailing behind watchfully.

Wherever Casey was, I couldn't help feeling sorry for her.

"This table is open," James announced.

Christine and I got up and made way for the next shift. We cashed in, and I had won over ten thousand dollars.

"Win?" she asked, as we walked to the bar.

"Yes."

"So did I."

"So did he," I observed.

A lot of the money we had won belonged to the other players in the game.

We sat at the bar and ordered drinks. When they came we clinked glasses and drank.

"That last pot made you the big winner, I think."

"I guess it did," I agreed.

"Think we impressed him?"

I honestly wasn't sure.

"I don't think anything impresses him," I told her.

"Oh, I'm not so sure. He reacted when you raised sixty-five hundred."

"Did he?" I asked innocently.

"Nick?"

"Hmm?"

"You never looked at your hole card, did you?"

"Sure I did," I told her, then added, "when everyone else did."

She shook her head.

"You're nuts."

"You don't impress anyone by going out," I said.

"No, I guess not, but you won, you rat, with a lousy deuce in the hole."

I shrugged and reminded her, "That's the game."

"What say we go up to my room and play a different one?" she proposed.

It sounded good to me.

"You're on."

Outside her room, as she was inserting the key in the lock I said, "Wait a minute."

She stopped, eyeing me quizzically.

"Is this going to cost me anything? I've had enough excitement for one night."

"Sweetheart," she said, opening the door and grabbing my tie, "you haven't begun to get excited."

CHAPTER TWENTY

Over breakfast in Christine's room the following morning she asked me, "What do you do now?"

I shrugged. "I'll have to find another way in. How about you?"

"I guess I'll move on, find another game. There are a couple of big ones I know of. If he doesn't want to invite me off of last night's game, I can't twist his arm," she told me fatalistically.

It was too bad I couldn't exhibit the same attitude, but since Casey's plan had failed and I had been unable to suitably impress the guy last night, I had to find some other way of getting inside his house.

As we were finishing our coffee there was a knock on her door.

"Are you shy?" I asked her, pointing to the bedroom, indicating that I was perfectly willing to hide in there if she so desired.

"Don't be an ass," she told me and went to answer the door. It was a bellboy with a long box. She took the box, told him to wait, and got him a tip—although the sight of her in her filmy negligee should have been tip enough for any man. He smiled at both of us—wide enough to split his face—and said thank you. She opened the box, revealing a dozen long-stemmed roses.

"Nick, you sweet thing," she exclaimed, picking one up from the box and smelling it.

"Sweetheart, I would love to take credit for those, if only to keep your opinion of me intact, but unfortunately I can't," I admitted.

"They're not from you?" she asked.

I shook my head.

"When would I have had time?" I asked. "I was with you all night. Don't you remember?"

"Oh, I remember that very well," she assured me, leaning over and planting a light kiss on my mouth. "Well then," she went on, standing up, "if they're not from you, who are they from?"

"May I take this opportunity to suggest that there is usually a card enclosed?"

She smiled at me sweetly and looked through the box, finding the card underneath the flowers. She opened it and read it.

"Nick, I've got good news and bad news."

"What's the good news?"

"The roses are from Oswaldo Orantes. He would like me to come to his home this evening for a private poker game."

"Good for you," I said smiling halfheartedly. I was glad for her, but I had to admit that I was a little irked at the fact that she had impressed him and I had not. It also bothered me that I cared whether I had impressed him or not.

"And the bad news?"

She made a show of looking through the box further, then said, "There's no card for you, love."

I smiled and replied, "Very funny."

She laughed, put the single rose back in the box with the others, and came to sit in my lap.

"Really," she began, putting arms around my neck, "I'm sorry you didn't get invited, but maybe I can help you."

"Oh? How?"

She shrugged.

"Tell me what you want from Orantes's house. Maybe I can get it for you."

I regarded her expression critically. It was sexy, it was innocent, and it was persuasive. I was suddenly suspicious of her motives, suspicious of her for the first time since the shooting incident on the float. That could have been a set-up to get me to trust her, but who could she be working with? The Specialist had always worked alone—up until now.

"Well?" she prodded.

"I can't say until I check with my client," I hedged. "If I decide that you can help me, I'll let you know."

She frowned and asked me straight out, "Are you suspicious of me for some reason?"

"Yes."

"Why?"

"It's part of my business to be suspicious. If I wasn't, I wouldn't be very good at what I do."

"It must be terrible for you to have to be like that all the time."

"Some days it's rougher than others."

She took her arms from around my neck and put her hands flat against my chest.

"Nick, I was only offering to help you. If you can't readily accept, then forget it."

She spoke without anger, without a trace of rancor. She watched me, waiting for my reaction.

"Okay," I agreed, "it's forgotten."

She slapped my chest with both hands, saying, "Oh, you're bad," in an exasperated tone.

"I know," I agreed. I slapped her on the rump and

said, "I think I'd better get dressed."

She slid from my lap, and I got up and walked to the bedroom.

"How's your ankle?" she called out.

The question surprised me, because I hadn't thought about my ankle since yesterday. In fact, I realized just then that I had left my cane in my room the previous night. The ankle, and foot for that matter, felt surprisingly good.

"It's okay," I called back, getting my clothes on. I needed a shower, but I'd take that in my own room.

When I reentered the other room she was having another cup of coffee, and rereading Orantes's card.

I walked over to her and held out the envelope with the money the waiter had given me last night.

"What's this?" she asked, looking at it.

"It's the money you lent me last night. It really came in handy there at the end. Thanks, I appreciate it."

She looked at me with a funny expression and asked, "Nick, what on earth are you talking about?"

She was convincing, so convincing that I believed her.

"When I took that break last night, you didn't send a waiter after me with an envelope?"

"I did not," she assured me.

"Then who did?"

"Who sent me the roses?"

"Orantes?" I asked. I thought it over, then shook my head. "That doesn't scan. Why would he?"

"I'm sure I don't know."

I tapped the envelope against my other hand, then returned it to my pocket. Leaning over, I kissed her on the forehead and said, "I'm genuinely pleased that you got what you wanted, Christine."

She kissed me on the mouth, holding my face between her hands and answered, "Thank you, Nick. So am I."

"Don't worry about me."

"Oh, I won't."

"I'll muddle through."

"I don't doubt it. I imagine that you can be very resourceful when you have to be."

"You're too kind."

I touched her cheek and started for the door. When I reached it I turned around and said her name.

"Yes, love?"

"I wish I had sent you the roses."

There were no flowers when I returned to my room, but someone had taken the trouble to force an envelope beneath my door. I picked it up and carried it with me to the bathroom. I set the temperature of my shower water, undressed, then sat on the commode while the room filled with steam. I opened the envelope.

It was an invitation from Orantes to participate in a private poker game at his home that evening.

I left the note on the counter and took a long shower.

CHAPTER TWENTY-ONE

After the shower I called the number Al Nuss had given me inside the hotel, and the phone was picked up by a girl.

"Is Al there?"

"Who's calling?" she asked in a sleepy voice.

"Tell him it's Nick."

"Just a minute."

She dropped the phone, and in a few moments it was picked up by Nuss.

"Kind of early," he told me.

"I'm sorry to interrupt, but I need to know if any flowers were delivered this morning to the bridal suite."

"What?"

I repeated my request.

"You're a strange bird, Nick. You playing games with the new bride?"

"Al, could we forget the questions?"

"Okay, okay. When do you need to know?"

"Five minutes ago."

He sighed into the phone and said, "I'll get back to you."

It took ten minutes.

"A box was delivered to the bridal suite about forty minutes ago."

"What was in it?" I wanted to see if he was really working for his money. He was.

"Roses, a dozen, long-stemmed."

"And a card."

"Yes."

"From who?"

"They were sent by the man on the hill. Is that what you wanted to know?"

"Yes. Thanks, Al. Put it on my tab."

"I'll start page two," he promised, and hung up.

Casey had been invited to Orantes's house, but not for poker. Was she also invited for tonight?

I decided to ask her.

I changed into a bathing suit and sent down to the veranda. I ordered a Bloody Mary and waited. Casey came by half an hour later without Mr. Tremayne.

When she joined me I asked, "Where's the boy wonder?"

"He'll be down soon. I figured you'd be waiting, so I came ahead."

"You figured?"

"I want to know what you were doing last night."

"Me? I never kiss and tell."

"I mean before that."

"I was playing cards."

"I know that!" she snapped, then looked around to see if anyone had heard. "What were you doing at the high stakes table?" she continued in a softer but no less demanding tone.

I decided to level with her.

"I knew that Orantes was a gambler. I thought that if your plan failed, I might impress him enough to wangle an invitation to a private game."

"How did you find out about his gambling?"

"I asked around."

"You're backup, Nick," she reminded me.

"Does that mean I'm not supposed to know anything that you and Mr. Tremayne don't choose to tell me?" I asked. Shaking my head I answered my own question. "No, I keep my ears open, I ask a few discreet questions, and I shed a little light on this darkness I'm in."

"Nobody's keeping you in the dark," she insisted.

We sat silent for a few moments.

"I didn't see him look at me once last night. Did you?"

"No," I admitted.

"But he did, I know he did."

"Do you think it's impossible for a man not to look at you?" I asked.

She leaned back in her chair and raised her chin. She was wearing a two-piece bathing suit, and it hid very little.

"What do you think?"

"Difficult, I admit, but not impossible."

Her lips tightened and her nostrils flared.

"Well, I've got news for you. This morning I received a dozen roses and an invitation to visit Mr. Orantes at his home this evening."

"Did the invitation include your husband?"

She didn't answer.

"How are you getting there?"

"He's sending a car."

I wondered if it was the same car he was sending to pick up Christine and me, or if we were all to get separate cars.

"What time?"

"Seven."

Ah-ha. Two hours ahead of me. I imagined that Christine's card must have also said nine o'clock, since we were both going to play poker. That meant that Casey would be inside without any cover for at least two hours.

Dinner, I figured, would be on the agenda. And after that?

"Be careful, Casey," I told her.

Her face softened and she leaned forward, almost put her hand over mine, then thought better of it and snatched it back.

"Don't worry, Nick. I'm a pro."

"Yeah, well, pros get killed, too. Don't get cocky with him," I warned.

"I won't," she promised.

"What will Allan be doing while you're . . . away?"

She hesitated, then decided to go ahead and tell me.

"He'll be monitoring me in our room. I'll be carrying a bug."

"Where?"

"Where he won't find it, no matter what," she assured me.

I believed her. They were making them incredibly small these days.

"What will you be doing tonight?" she asked.

"Me?" I asked, then finished my drink before answering. "I'm going to be playing poker."

CHAPTER TWENTY-TWO

By the time I had finished my shower, I'd decided that it was time for Nick Carter to come out of the dark. To do so, I decided to step right into the lion's den.

I was going to go and see Oswaldo Orantes.

It was time for me to start working the way I worked best—alone, which, in a sense, I was. Hawk had kept me in the dark when he briefed me, although I did feel that he had been trying to warn me to watch my ass. Casey and Trumball weren't telling me everything either. As far as the Specialist was concerned, he was on my tail, but he was playing games, which was very odd. Although we had never met, I thought I knew him pretty well, and this behavior was way out of character for him.

As for Christine, she had succeeded in making me suspicious of her motives for being on Pleasure Island, and Al Nuss just didn't fit in at all.

It was time for me to take the offensive, to go out and find some answers for myself.

Orantes was the man who could supply a lot of these answers. I was going to have to go and see him with a good enough cover story so that he would open up to me.

So far, neither Christine nor the team of Casey and

Trumball knew that I would be present at Orantes's home that evening, and I could see nothing constructive in letting them in on it before then.

What none of them knew, including the man with the invitations, was that I was inviting myself up to the house this morning for breakfast as well.

I called the desk and made arrangements for a car to be waiting in front of the hotel—and I specified that it be a different make and model from the one I'd used previously. There was no point in making myself easy to spot from the roof of the hotel.

The car was out front when I came down and I retraced the same route I had taken two days before. When I reached that point where I had stopped to climb the hill and inspect the wall, I kept on going. About two hundred yards further on, the road made a sharp turn to the left, and coming out of the turn I could see the front gates of Orantes's island estate.

I pulled up to the gate and got out of the car. As I approached the wrought iron entrance, a man similar in appearance to Orantes's two bodyguards the night before—they must have had a sale when he bought them in bunches—also approached, but from the inside. He was wearing a sidearm in plain sight, a large .45 that would probably kill my car if he fired into it.

"Can I help you?" he asked.

"I hope so," I replied. "I'd like to see Mr. Orantes."

"Have you an appointment?" I hadn't heard the two bodyguards speak the night before, but this one spoke with a slight Spanish accent. I wondered if all of Orantes's people were Hispanic.

"I'm afraid I don't," I admitted, "but I believe Mr. Orantes will consent to see me."

"And what leads you to believe this?" he asked as if genuinely interested.

I showed him the letter inviting me to the house that

evening for the private poker game.

He handed it back, seemingly unimpressed.

"This letter states that you are invited at nine this evening, and that an automobile will be sent for you. Are you not a bit early, *señor?*" he asked politely.

I accepted the letter back through the gate and answered, "Indeed, yes, I am early, but this visit has nothing to do with poker. Would you be kind enough to inform Mr. Orantes of my presence, and tell him that I am a prospective buyer for the item he is interested in selling?"

He thought a moment, then nodded to himself as if he had just made a momentous decision.

"You will wait here, please," he instructed.

"I won't go anywhere," I promised.

He disappeared from view. I assumed there was a gatehouse or at least a phone he could use to call the big house.

While I waited I turned and looked out to sea. From this part of the island there was nothing visible other than a clear blue sky and a deep blue sea. The hotel was on the opposite side of the island and unless the Specialist had developed bullets that could turn corners, I wasn't in any danger of being shot at again by him or anyone else from the hotel.

Still, my back itched just a little.

After about three minutes, the man returned to the gates and opened them to allow me to enter.

"My car," I told him.

"Your car will be cared for, rest assured. Mr. Orantes has consented to see you, but he allows no strange automobiles on the grounds. You will follow this road, please. It is a bit of a walk, but I assure you it is not an endless journey."

"Thank you," I said and started walking up the road, feeling a little like Dorothy without Toto.

Once again, without conscious thought, I had left my cane behind in my room. I tried walking without favoring my injured foot and ankle, and was pleasantly surprised to find that it responded well. There was no pain or discomfort at all. I'd be fine as long as I didn't have to run any hundred-yard dashes—downhill.

I was glad that the guard had assured me that the walk wasn't endless, but I was beginning to doubt it when the house finally came into view. On the massive front steps I could see one of the big man's bodyguards, who I recognized from the night before, waiting for me. As I ascended the steps, he opened the large, oak front door and said, "Mr. Orantes is waiting on the patio."

"Thank you."

He followed me in, shut the door behind us, then took the lead, saying, "Follow me, please." He, too, had a Spanish accent, so I guessed that Orantes wasn't an equal opportunity employer.

I followed him down a long hall that was lined with closed doors until we reached a set of French doors leading outside.

As we passed through the doors I saw a large swimming pool, unused at the moment, and beyond it I could see Orantes sitting on a patio in a padded armchair. The house extended completely around the pool and patio, so that I was completely boxed in from all sides.

The second bodyguard was seated behind Orantes in a normal patio chair, sipping from a cup I assumed held coffee.

"Mr. Collins," Orantes greeted me without rising, "welcome to my home." As well as not rising, neither did he extend his hand to be shaken. Instead he used a massive paw to indicate the patio chair opposite him.

"Please, be seated. Will you have breakfast? Some coffee or tea?"

"Just coffee will be fine," I told him. "Thank you."

I noticed that the patio table was pushed off in a corner. Obviously, Orantes would have a hell of a time getting his legs under it, so I guessed it was only used for guests, while he reclined in a large, padded armchair. Had I agreed to breakfast, he probably would have had the table set between us.

"José," he said, speaking to the man who had escorted me from the front door, "have Louisa bring another cup, and a fresh pot of coffee." To me he said, "The coffee is Columbian. You will enjoy it."

It sounded like an order.

If he himself had any trace of a Spanish accent, he hid it well with practiced skill.

José disappeared through a second set of French doors behind the patio.

"Now, Mr. Collins, while we await the fresh coffee, please tell me to what I owe this unexpected visit, hmm?" He made the word *unexpected* sound more like the word *uninvited*. He was being extremely polite, however, so I answered in kind.

"I hope you will forgive the intrusion, Mr. Orantes, but I felt impelled to make you aware of my reason for being here on Pleasure Island."

He wrinkled his nose at the mention of the resort's name, a curiously delicate gesture for a man so large.

"Disgusting, is it not, what they call my island now? Ah, but I suppose it does attract the tourists," he added resignedly. The only hint that English may not have been his first language was the precise way he spoke it.

He produced a cigar—a Havana, naturally—from within his jacket, and the bodyguard seated behind him was immediately there with a lighter.

Once he had the cigar glowing to his satisfaction, Orantes continued.

"So tell me, then, why you have come to my island if not simply to gamble—which you do very well, I might add. I was quite impressed last night with both you and the young lady, ah, Miss Hall, was it not?"

"Yes, Christine Hall."

He was pleased with himself for remembering.

"It is rare that I find two new players—new to me, that is—in the same evening, at the same table, who both impress me to the degree that I would invite them to one of my private little sessions."

"I appreciate the invitation," I assured him.

"You and Miss Hall are, ah, acquainted?" he asked.

"We are."

"You are old friends, perhaps?"

"I'm afraid not. We've only just become acquainted since I arrived on the island a couple of days ago."

"Ah, I see. A lovely woman, is she not?"

"She is that," I agreed.

He seemed to look inward at that remark and said, "A pity she isn't a blonde," while shaking his head.

"I beg your pardon?"

"Blondes. I'm afraid I have an incurable weakness for blond women," he explained.

"I've heard of worse weaknesses."

"I'm sure."

At that point Louisa arrived with the extra cup and the fresh pot of coffee, followed closely by José. For some reason I almost expected Louisa to be a young blonde, but she was the original duenna: portly, elderly, with her hair up in a bun.

"*Gracias*, Louisa," he told her.

"*Por nada, señor.*"

She left and José did the pouring. He handed me a cup, then Orantes. After that, he walked to the patio table and put the pot down.

I tasted the coffee and found that Orantes was right; it was delicious.

"Well, Mr. Collins, enough idle chatter for the moment. You told my man something about buying an item I have to sell. What was that about, please?"

"Oh, I think you know what it's about, Mr. Orantes. You put the word out that you have, to use your words, 'an item' to sell, and that you are holding a private auction this week. I've simply arrived early and wanted to let you know I was here. I also did not want to enter your house this evening under false pretenses."

"Commendable," he nodded, "very much so. However, with the ability you have to play poker, your entry into my home this evening would not have been construed as a false pretense, I assure you."

"I appreciate that."

"Who is your principal in this matter?" he asked.

"I really don't believe that's pertinent—unless my bid is the high one, of course. At that time I will reveal for whom I am dealing."

He nodded and said, "Satisfactory."

"Unless we can work out a private arrangement—"

He cut me off with a shake of his head and a wave of a massive hand.

"If you know anything about me—" he began, then paused to see if I would react. When I didn't, he continued, "—you know that I never deal privately. It cuts my profits."

"I understand," I told him, making myself sound disappointed.

"I like to think that I am a very fair man, Mr. Collins. I exhibited that last night, I think."

It took me a moment to realize what he was referring to.

"Ah, you mean when you instructed James to hold my seat at the table while I took a break."

"Suggested, not instructed," he corrected me, "but yes, that is what I mean. You had a streak of incredibly bad luck, but you were smart enough to know how to overcome it. You play the game very well, but you are also very daring."

"Daring?"

"The final hand. You never looked at your hole card," he pointed out.

I smiled and said, "You noticed. It was the final hand," I said by way of explanation.

"I understand."

I finished my coffee and while I was looking for somewhere to put the cup, José came over and took it from me. I thanked him, and he gave me a curt nod of his head and put the cup next to the pot, on the table. Then he crossed his hands in front of him and kept his eyes on me. I knew he'd go from waiter to bodyguard in one second flat if I made a move at his boss.

"About this, uh, item you're selling, Mr. Orantes—"

Again the head shake and the hand wave.

"I will not speak of it further. You are welcome here this evening, but only to play poker."

This time I was the one who said, "I understand. Thank you for the invitation."

"Don't thank me. I invited you out here for purely selfish reasons. Tell me, would you like to ride out in the same car with Miss Hall?"

I thought a moment before answering, "I don't think so. I would appreciate it, as a matter of fact, if you would have me picked up first, say at eight forty-five. Would that be possible?" I asked.

He spread his hands magnanimously. "I don't see why not. Is this a superstition of some sort?"

That was as good a reason as any, and one a gambler could understand.

"Just a small one. I'd appreciate your indulgence in the matter," I told him.

"No problem," he assured me. "Would you like another cup of coffee?"

I shook my head. "It was very good, but I've had enough, thanks."

"Then I must ask you to leave. I have other matters to attend to today. Until tonight, then?"

I recognized I was being dismissed and stood up.

"Thank you for your hospitality."

"And thank you for your honesty. José, show Mr. Collins out, please."

"Yes, sir."

I started to follow José, then turned and said, "There is one more thing."

"Yes?" he asked patiently.

I approached him and said, "Forgive me for asking, but do I understand that you are having a guest for dinner this evening?"

He frowned and answered, "I am."

"A young blond woman who is in fact occupying the bridal suite at the hotel?"

He paused a moment, then answered, "That is correct, but how is it you know this? And why is it your business?"

"I guess it isn't, not really," I admitted, "but I understand that her young husband is very jealous."

"I have no fear of husbands, Mr. Collins, young or otherwise. The lady is free to accept or decline my invitation. I will send my car to pick her up. Whether or not she uses it is quite up to her. As for her husband, I'm sure that will be her problem, not mine—or yours," he told me pointedly.

"I agree."

"Then I don't see where this concerns you, Mr. Collins. Have you a reason for prying into my personal affairs?"

The bodyguard in the chair behind him was starting to get twitchy.

"I was just worried about the, uh, item that you have

to sell—" I began.

"The item is quite safe, Mr. Collins."

"Well, it's just that there may be some factions who are not as fair-minded as you are."

He began laughing.

"You mean, someone might try to steal it?" he asked. "Mr. Collins, my security here is excellent. There is no way anyone could get in here to steal that, uh, item."

He was very sure of himself.

"Not unless you invite them," I told him, then turned to follow José out.

CHAPTER TWENTY-THREE

I figured that I had given Orantes sufficient food for thought concerning Casey, but suppose my parting remark backfired? Suppose he became suspicious of me? I didn't think that would be the case, however. He had to feel that I had opened up to him, been honest about my reasons for being on Pleasure Island. He'd have to take into account the fact that I didn't have to announce myself the way I had just done.

Would he become suspicious of Casey, though?

I hoped so. I hoped he would think about it just enough to keep an eye on her the entire time she was there, thereby preventing her from making her switch.

Casey was continuing to worry me. She wasn't operting the way I would expect her to. It was as if there were something else on her mind. Granted, I felt as if she and Trumball were trying to keep me in the background—and I didn't appreciate that—but I was also concerned with her getting caught if she wasn't operating at peak efficiency. If Orantes watched her closely enough and she never got a chance to try the switch, then there would be no chance of her being caught.

The other thing was the information itself. If it was really as important as everyone thought, then I wasn't going to leave it to two baby agents to grab. I wasn't going to stand back and watch them muff it. They were ill-prepared for an assignment like this, so I was going to be the one to grab the notes. I may not have been the agent-in-charge on this thing, but I was ranking agent, and I was making my decision based on experience.

I had an in to Orantes's house, now, on two counts. I was hoping I could get him to be magnanimous enough to give his poker guests a tour of his house before the game. People who own plush homes are usually very eager to show them off. From a tour I might be able to figure out where he was holding the notes. Once I knew where they were, that was half the battle.

I still had some reconnoitering to do, however, before I walked into Orantes's house with larceny on my mind.

There were two ways of getting out of the house once I had the papers I was after: by land or by sea. I knew what the grounds were like, so I had to take a look at what the seaward side of the house looked like. That meant I had to rent a boat from the resort and take a ride around the island.

I turned in the car and entered the lobby with the intention of returning to my room. As I started for the elevators I saw something that made me stop short. Actually, I saw someone, an old friend—or an old enemy. I've never been quite sure which one Kevin Joseph James Bagley really was.

Kevin was English on his father's side, American on his mother's, and greedy all on his own. His patriotic loyalties—for want of a better phrase—went to whoever paid the highest price.

He was standing at the desk registering, and I knew that Kevin Bagley had never taken a vacation in his life. He called them "counterproductive." That could mean only one thing.

Kevin was on Pleasure Island to bid at Orantes's auction.

There was one problem with that. Kevin knew my face, and he knew my real name. He also knew what business I was in.

He could blow my cover sky high, and he would if he thought he could turn a profit by doing it.

I couldn't very well play hide and seek with him for the entire time we were both on the island, and I had better things to do and much more to worry about without adding Kevin Bagley to my list.

There was really only one way to play it, and I plunged in.

I walked straight to the front desk and got there just as he was turning around. When he saw me his eyes widened momentarily and then so did his mouth, into a smile. Kevin Bagley had the whitest teeth I'd ever seen and more of them than anyone I'd ever known—or so it seemed. He was tall and seemed slim unless you knew that beneath all that clothing were hidden whipcord muscles. I'd opposed Kevin many times but never physically. It would be quite a challenge.

I made it a point to speak before he did.

"Buy you a drink?" I offered.

"Smashing," he answered. His British accent was a tool he used, turning it on and off as he pleased.

He tried to say something, but I shook him off. Neither of us spoke until we were seated in the bar with our drinks before us.

"Shall we introduce ourselves, old boy?" Kevin asked, realizing that we had never encountered each other while using our real names.

"Capital idea," I said, extending my hand. "I'm Nick Collins, a college professor."

"Professor?" he asked, then started to laugh. "You? A college professor?"

"I see you find that amusing."

"My dear man, that's like putting the sheep in the

charge of the wolf. The chickens in the hands of the fox. The—"

"I get the picture," I assured him.

"Well, then, it's my turn. I am Joseph James, vacationing playboy."

"It suits you."

"Thank you."

"Except for one thing."

He frowned. "What's that?"

I leaned forward and whispered, "You've never taken a vacation in your life."

He nodded and said, "That's true."

"I could tell you that I'm here for the sun and the sand and the girls, but you wouldn't buy that, would you, Nick?" he asked.

"No more than you would about me."

"I'm afraid you've got that right, old boy."

"So I guess we're both here for the same reason."

"I suppose so, although it surprises me that you would be sent simply to bid on some pieces of paper. You'd be more likely to be sent along to nick it, wouldn't you?" he asked, kidding, then he developed the kind of look you get on your face when you've suddenly understood the punchline of an involved joke.

In jest, he'd just about hit the nail on the head.

"You're not serious?"

"I didn't say anything."

"Come on, Nick, old boy, we've gone round an' round too many times in the past to play games with each other now. You're going to try to cop the bob from right under the big man's nose. What's your in?" he asked eagerly.

I wondered how Kevin was being paid on this, and by whom? Naturally, he'd be getting some kind of a flat fee for his services, but he must have been guaranteed a bonus if he delivered the goods. If I stole the notes from

Orantes, I knew he'd try to grab them from me, pocket the money he'd been given to make his bid with, and also collect his bonus.

When I didn't answer, Kevin went on and answered his own question.

"I've got it! You've been a dabbler at gambling yourself, haven't you, Nick—I mean, other than with your life." He leaned across the table and asked in a low voice, "You've gotten yourself invited to one of his private games, haven't you?"

"You're doing all the talking, Kevin."

"Talking, hell. I'm here to gamble, Nick, one way or another. I've got an invitation, too—for tonight, as a matter of fact. When are you going?"

I decided to play it straight with him—to a point.

"Tonight," I admitted.

"That's grand, lad! It'll be a pleasure taking your money."

"Another drink?"

"Sure."

We called the waiter and reordered.

If Kevin had done the same thing I did, wangled an invitation to Orantes's game, I wondered how many others might have done the same. How many of the people I would be playing poker with that night would also be there to bid on the notes?

And what about Christine? Could she also be a potential buyer? Also, was anyone else intending to steal the stuff instead of buying it?

Then another question hit me, one for Casey. Was the United States government sending someone to bid on the notes as a cover for our assignment?

When we had our fresh drinks Kevin asked, "You going to snatch the bob tonight?"

"I haven't said I'm going to snatch it at all, Kevin," I reminded him.

"Oh, don't worry, Nick, old boy, I won't get in your way. I'd much rather take it from you than from Orantes. That way I get to keep the bid money, collect a bonus—and I get to go one-up on you."

He'd been trying to one-up me for years and saw this as a possible opportunity to do it.

The funny thing was, I was entertaining the thought of teaming up with Kevin. I preferred working with him to working with Casey and Trumball. I knew Kevin, I knew how his mind worked, and I knew what he was capable of.

I was sure that with Kevin's help I could boost the notes from Orantes's house. Then all I would have to worry about was keeping it from him.

At that point, Casey came walking into the bar, obviously looking for either Trumball or me. When she spotted me she walked over, saying, "Nick, I—" then stopped short when she didn't recognize the man I was with.

"Casey, I'd like you to meet a friend of mine," I said, rising. Kevin also got up from his seat like a proper English gentleman, eyeing Casey with obvious admiration. "This is Joseph James. Joe is what you call a playboy."

"Now, Nick," Kevin scolded me. He had big eyes for Casey and put on a show for her. He took her hand, bowed low, and kissed it expertly.

She reacted the way most women would. She became a little flustered but was pleased by the attention.

"Hello, Mr. James."

"Please, call me Joe—and won't you join us for a drink?"

"Well, I'm supposed to meet my husband—" she began, but Kevin was good-looking and charming, and after all, she wasn't really married.

"Husband?" Kevin said, exhibiting surprise. "Please, tell me it isn't true."

"I'm afraid it is," she told him, reacting to his well-practiced charm, "but I will have a drink, after all."

"Splendid," he said, holding her chair for her.

She sat, and we ordered again. This was to be my last, if I had any intention of driving a boat and doing it in a straight line.

"Are you here for pleasure, Mr.—I mean, Joe?"

It seemed a stock question on the island.

"Why else would anyone come here?" he answered. "I'm a gambler as well as a playboy, Casey."

"You're the first playboy I've ever met who admitted he was one," she told him.

"How many have you known?" I asked her.

She gave me a dirty look. I had made her realize that she was reacting to Kevin's charm. She sipped her drink and put it down.

"I'm sorry, I've really got to meet Allan."

"Allan?" Kevin asked.

"Her husband," I supplied.

"Oh, the lucky man."

She smiled at him, then saw me watching and ditched it.

"Thank you both for the drink," she said and hurried off. I think she might have forgotten what she wanted to see me about.

"That's her, huh?" Kevin asked.

"Who?"

"Your backup."

"Other way around," I told him, shaking my head.

"You're the backup?" He frowned at me and added, "That's hard to buy, Nick. She's a baby."

"I got hurt a while back, but wanted to stay in circulation," I explained. "They sent me to babysit her and her partner."

"The husband?"

I nodded.

"I thought you were favoring your foot a bit," he observed.

"It's just not your style to act as backup man."

"I couldn't agree with you more and I think that's about to change."

"What does that mean?"

"That means that maybe we can work something out, Kevin, that'll do us both a lot of good."

I decided to play his game for a while. It had nothing to do with pride or ego. I had given the assignment a fair chance, and Casey and Allan just weren't right for the job. I decided I could do better on my own with a little help from my so-called friend. It was risky to bet on Kevin, but for some reason I felt safer gambling on him then on the other two.

CHAPTER TWENTY-FOUR

The water felt good, cool, and refreshing as the fine spray covered my face and bare chest.

I had rented a small powerboat from the hotel and was running it around a bit to get the feel of it before proceeding with it to the other side of the island.

The ride was also giving me some time to sort out all that had happened up until now. Things were starting to get more complicated, what with me being in the dark all the time and new characters running in and out of what was quickly becoming a farce of an assigment.

It had all started with Hawk handing me one of the strangest assignments of my career. In effect he had told me to go to Pleasure Island and run around in the dark. Ostensibly, I was to babysit two young agents setting up a snatch of some important information, but something was definitely rotten in Denmark—and on Pleasure Island.

Okay, so that was me.

Now I had to deal with two young agents who I knew briefly four years ago: Casey Laurence, with whom I had shared some moments to remember, and Allan Trumball, with whom I had shared some moments better forgotten. Trumball was an ass four years ago, and he was still an ass now. Casey, however, had shown some real promise then, but her actions since my arrival on the island were, at best, suspect.

Oswaldo Orantes was the man who held the information we were after, and he intended to sell it to the highest bidder. Were we here to bid? No, we were here to steal, without letting it be known that we had stolen. This was to be accomplished by stealing the notes and replacing them with phony ones. This information was given to me by Casey, but I wasn't supposed to know all of that because I was just the backup man.

Add to this lineup one smart cookie from New York named Al Nuss, who was running a racket or two on Pleasure Island with seemingly unlimited resources; Christine Hall, a poker-playing beauty who just might be after more than an inside straight; and Kevin Joseph James Bagley, a soldier of fortune acting as buyer for only-he-knew-who, but whose loyalties were to folding green, no matter where it came from.

If he thought he could make more cash helping me steal the stuff, he'd do it.

At the moment all of these people were running around Pleasure Island, and any one of them could possibly be the assassin known as the Specialist, who had my name next on his fatal dance card.

The Specialist. Now there was something odd. He had me in his sights twice and let me off the hook, a game he didn't have a reputation for playing.

I intended to make him sorry he had decided to play it with me.

There was a joker in this deck, too: Colonel James J. Lamb, who just might have been the man who had gotten me plunked down in the middle of this menagerie in the first place.

For what purpose?

Maybe to get me killed.

So what was I up to now?

I was throwing a monkey wrench into everybody's plans. Casey and Trumball thought they were going to pull a switch with the notes, but they were wrong. I was taking the stuff, with or without their help or the help of Kevin Bagley and despite anyone's efforts to the contrary.

I was coming out of the dark, one way or another.

Also, I was going to nail the Specialist, because I knew he wouldn't stop until he got me. Sooner or later, we'd square off, just as soon as he figured out how he wanted to face me. I was willing to wait for him to decide, because I'd be ready, injured foot or not.

As a matter of fact, the foot was feeling fine, but I had no intentions of testing it until the time came. The last thing I wanted to do was take a chance on reinjuring it before then.

Leaving the hotel bar, Kevin had tried to pump me about what I had meant by working something out, but I wasn't all that sure yet, so I put him off. We parted company so he could get settled, and I picked up my messages at the desk.

There were two, one from Casey, which she probably left after leaving the bar. She said she had something very important to talk to me about. The second message was from Christine, who simply wanted me to call her.

I'd answer both after my boat ride.

I was sorry that I had to become suspicious of Christine. If she was nothing more than what she appeared to be, then liking her was no problem . . . and I did like her. I hoped she was really just a lady who liked her gambling, and perhaps wanted a little more excitement in her life.

The boat started to feel pretty good to me, so I straightened her out and headed for the other side of the island. It was a short ride in a fast boat, and before long there was the big house on the hill, only from where I was it was at the top of a cliff.

At the base of the cliff was a dock where two boats were tied. One was a sixty-five-footer a family of six could live in comfortably; the other was a toy, something to go out and run around in; it was fast.

I throttled down but didn't stop. I thought that would be too conspicuous. I halved my speed and used the binoculars I had found in a footlocker on the boat. I could make out the front of the house where, that morning, I had been standing looking out to sea. As I circled around, I could see that there was another gate in the side of the wall. Had I driven past the front gate and around the bend further, I would have come to it. Instead, I had driven back to the hotel the way I had come.

There was a steep stairway that went up the cliff from the dock, which would leave you on the roadway across from that side gate.

If I grabbed the notes and couldn't get off the grounds through the front gate, I'd have to try the side gate. It wouldn't hurt to have a boat at that dock that could be used to get away.

The dock was large enough to accommodate a couple of more boats, about the size of the one I was in, so I intended to keep the idea in mind.

Even with the binoculars, I couldn't tell if there was a guard posted at that side gate, as there had been at the front one. I did notice, however, that this gate was not as big as the one in front. I doubted that it was large enough to drive a car through, so if I was going to get out by car, it would have to be by the front entrance.

I'd have to find out a few things before I made my final plans: whether there was a guard on that gate; where the keys to the two boats at the dock were kept; and if there was a third gate in the wall that extended entirely around the house.

I put down the binoculars and pushed up the speed again, circling around to head back to the hotel.

I had a couple of messages to answer.

CHAPTER TWENTY-FIVE

When I got back to my room I called Christine. She quickly made it clear why she had left me a message.

"I thought we might have lunch together," she told me, "but I guess you had other plans."

"Nothing exciting. I went for a boat ride."

"Alone?"

"All alone," I assured her.

"Nick?"

"Yes?"

"I'm sorry about tonight. I wish—"

"Don't start that again, Chris," I scolded her. "You're getting just what you wanted, and I'm glad."

"I know you are, that's why I—"

"That's why you what?"

She paused, then finished with, "That's why I care about you so much."

Ignore it, Carter, I told myself; it's just a momentary twinge of guilt.

"I feel the same, Christine."

"Let's have dinner together this evening, before I go?" she asked.

"Sure, why not. We'll celebrate before you take Orantes for all he's worth."

"You're a dream, Nick. I'll meet you in the dining room at seven thirty."

"Make it seven and you've got a date."

"Seven it is. See you then."

I hung up, half wishing I had told her about my invitation. She'd be surprised as hell to see me at Orantes's, but I wouldn't have to explain until tomorrow—if I had to explain at all.

I rang Casey's room next, hoping like hell Trumball wouldn't pick up. I was lucky; she answered the first ring.

"It's me, Case."

"I want to talk."

"So, talk."

"Not on the phone," she said firmly.

"The veranda?"

"No, not there either. Meet me on the roof of the hotel," she said as if she had just decided on that location.

"Why the roof?"

"It's where I want to—it's where we can be alone and not be overheard."

I'd been shot at twice at least and one of those times —I was sure—from that roof, but I agreed anyway. I didn't think it was a setup. Instinct, again. After all, Casey and I were on the same team—weren't we?

"Okay, Casey, on the roof. Will you be coming with or without your buddy?" I asked.

"I said I wanted us to be alone, Nick. Give me fifteen minutes."

"I'll be there," I assured her.

And I was.

First.

I left my room and immediately went to the roof. While I was there I checked the beach side of the roof and found the same markings on the ledge as I had found following the first shooting, as if a rifle had been mounted there. I also realized how right I had been about the float. It did look like a postage stamp from there. The Specialist was quite a shot.

"Nick," I heard Casey's voice call out from behind me. She sounded surprised. She had come up early, obviously meaning to be first, but I had beaten her there.

"Hi, Case. Same idea, huh?"

"I should have known you'd get here ahead of me. After all, you're still Nick Carter, aren't you?"

"I sure hope so. Take more than a bum ankle to change that, wouldn't it?"

She smiled and said, "A lot more."

"What's this about, Casey?"

She came over and stood next to me, looking down at the beach. It was packed with sun worshipers, three or four of whom had swum out to the float. In spite of myself, I was becoming more and more impressed with the Specialist.

"It's about Allan."

I frowned.

"What about him?"

"I'm worried about him. You being on this island has affected him, Nick. He hasn't been operating at peak efficiency since you arrived."

"Has he ever?" I asked, and then added to myself, neither have you.

"Nick—"

"Casey, is his dislike for me going to affect the outcome of this assignment?" I asked.

"I don't think so. I'm going to Orantes's house tonight at seven. I'll be wired, and Allan will be monitoring."

"What good will that do?"

"In case I get into trouble," she told me. "Allan will know."

"Then what?"

She looked at me strangely, and I knew she didn't have an answer. What was I doing here with these two? I asked myself.

"Forget that. Will you have the phony set of papers with you?" I asked her.

"Of couse."

I imagined that they were keeping the papers somewhere in their room. It was at that moment that I started thinking not only about stealing Orantes's papers, but Casey's set as well.

"Then if you don't expect the assignment to go wrong, what's this worry about Allan?"

She turned to face me and put her hands on my chest.

"It's you. I'm afraid that he's going to try to do something to you when this is over."

"I don't think he's that foolish, Casey," I told her.

"What do you mean?"

"He'd be no match for me, and he knows it."

"But that's part of it," she explained, "don't you see? You won't accept him as agent-in-charge, and he's jealous of you. All of these things are affecting him. He's not himself." She moved closer so that not only her hands but her breasts were up against my chest. "Nick, I think he's going to take a run at you. He wants to prove something to himself."

"And to you?"

She nodded, then admitted, "Yes, and to me. He loves me."

Her mouth was less than an inch from mine at that point, and she closed the remainder of the distance. Her lips were soft and her teeth were sharp as she bit into my lower lip.

"No kidding?" I asked.

"Don't make fun," she scolded. "He really isn't that bad, as long as I'm around to point him in the right direction."

"So, point him away from me. You're supposed to be able to handle him."

"I can—in most cases, but this . . . it's like an obsession, and it goes all the way back to training, when you humiliated him on the training course."

I shook my head in wonder at a grown man holding a grudge this long for such a ridiculous reason.

"Nick, I'm afraid. Please, don't kill him."

I looked at her in surprise.

"Oh, so it's him you're worried about, not me."

"Don't be silly. I don't want either of you killed," she insisted.

"Are you in love with Allan?" I asked her seriously.

"What a ridiculous notion," she scoffed.

Her hands went from my chest to up around my neck, and she pressed herself tightly against me. Our lips met and lingered pleasantly for some time.

"I don't love anyone, Nick," she told me, "but if I did . . . " she trailed off and kissed me again.

"Let's get off that subject," I suggested.

"For now?"

I nodded. "For now."

She backed off and gave me—gave us both—some breathing room.

"Okay, so you want to keep Allan and me from killing each other, is that about the size of it?"

"That's it," she answered. "You can do it, Nick. You're that much better than he is."

"Okay," I promised her, "if I can avoid it, I won't hurt him. After all, we're really all on the same side . . . aren't we?"

"Of course we are . . . but speaking of being on the same side, who's your good-looking friend?"

"Who?" I asked, then realized who she meant. For my own reasons I decided to tell her his real name. "You mean Joe James. His real name is Kevin—"

"Kevin . . ." she interrupted me saying the name half to herself. "Joseph, James—" she went on, saying the names separately. "Kevin Bagley! I've heard of him. Nick, what's he doing here?"

"What do you think?" I asked.

"He's here to bid," she guessed. I nodded. "Well, what does he think you're here for?"

"To bid, which reminds me."

"About what?"

"A question. Are our people sending anyone in to bid?"

"What for? We're going to steal the notes," she said— just to remind me.

"Yeah, but we don't want anyone to know we stole them, remember? Aren't we sending someone in to bid, just for show?"

She stared at me a moment, then admitted, "I don't know."

Agent-in-charge, huh? I thought.

"Never mind. Is that it? Meeting adjourned?"

"I guess."

"You've got to get set up for tonight, don't you? You've got to look your best for Orantes."

"I could have sworn he didn't take one look at me last evening," she admitted to me.

"Obviously he got by both of us with at least one glance," I told her. "But then, that would be all it would take for any man, wouldn't it?"

The compliment pleased her, and she rewarded me with another kiss.

"My plan will work, Nick. You'll see."

"I hope so, Casey, I hope so. Now you go ahead and get yourself ready."

"Tomorrow, this will all be finished, Nick, and then we can go home. Can we . . . see each other then?"

"Sure, why not?"

She smiled like a little girl who had just been given a promise, then left the roof.

Something was missing, and it took me a moment to figure out what it was.

When I had lied to Christine, I had felt a twinge of guilt. When I lied to Casey, there was no feeling of guilt at all.

I wondered why.

CHAPTER TWENTY-SIX

Casey's revelation was just what I needed. Now only did I have to worry about the Specialist, but now I had to keep an eye on her half-assed, half-witted partner as well.

I went back to my room, called the desk, and asked for Mr. James's room.

"Mr. James?" I asked when he answered.

"Yes?"

"This is Mr. Collins."

"Oh, hello, Mr. Collins. What can I do for you?"

"I thought we might continue our conversation of earlier today," I told him.

"Would that also include continuing our drinking as well?" he inquired.

"Of course."

"Then I'll meet you in the bar—"

"No, the veranda would be better. Say fifteen minutes?"

"That's fine. See you then."

Kevin was here on the island and I knew what to expect of him, so I decided to use him. Casey and Trumball were new to me and what I had seen so far was very unimpressive, so I figured the evil I knew was better than the evil I didn't respect. I was going to leave them in the dark as far as my plan was concerned—which was still only partly formed in my own mind. They wouldn't have appreciated it, anyway, since technically they were the agents-in-charge.

I was about to leave to meet Kevin when a thought struck me. It never hurt to be just a little too careful. I picked up the phone and called Al Nuss's number. There was no answer, so I called the desk and asked for him to be paged and put on the line. It took a few moments before he finally came on.

"Yeah, Nuss," he said.

"Al, it's Nick. I need some information."

"How much?"

"Just a small piece. I need to know if any calls have been made from room four-thirty-two today," I told him, giving him Kevin's room number.

"From when to when?"

"Just today. A guy named Joseph James registered this afternoon. Can you get me that while I hold on?"

"Sure. One sec."

It was a little more than that, give or take a minute, when he came back on the line.

"Okay, Nick, got it. No calls went through the hotel switchboard," he assured me.

"What about inside the hotel?"

"One call."

"To where?"

"The brida suite. Looks like that Mrs. Tremayne is attracting all kinds of attention, doesn't it?" he asked. He could've been talking about me and Kevin, and then again he could've also meant Orantes.

"Okay, Al, thanks."

"Don't mention it. Your bill is piling up."

"Don't worry about it. I'll see you."

So Kevin had called Casey's room. Well, that just gave me something else to talk to him about.

I went down and met him on the veranda. He was halfway through his first drink, and when he saw me he waved at the waiter signaling him to bring two more.

"I'll let you catch up," he told me, indicating that he'd nurse his first one until I finished mine.

"Kevin, I've decided to use you," I told him.

"You did? With or without my consent?" he asked, amused at my choice of words.

"With it. It's also going to make you a lot of money," I promised, not knowing whether or not I'd be able to keep such a promise.

"It will also put me in bad with the people I'm representing, won't it?"

"Not necessarily, not if it all works out right."

He thought a moment, then said, "Okay, mate, I'll listen."

"You've got to trust me, too, just a bit, okay? Again, it'll be worth it to you."

He narrowed his eyes and asked, "Am I going to end up having to kill you, Nick?"

I looked shocked and said, "I should hope not."

At that point the waiter came with the drinks, and we suspended conversation until he'd gone.

Kevin picked up his second drink, and I said, "I thought you were going to wait."

"I lied. Go ahead, I'm listening."

"Well, for tonight, I just want you to keep your eyes and ears open, at Orantes's house. I'm going to try to get him to give us a tour of his house. Go along with me, and if he goes for it, remember whatever you can about the layout. Between the two of us we should be able to get the place down pat."

"You going to make the swipe tonight?"

"If it's possible, but I don't think so. I think Orantes's special game is going to stretch until at least the day of the auction. Hell, we're here, and he's got to do something until then, so we'll all play poker.''

"Do you know any of the other players?"

"One. Christine Hall."

"The lady from Louisiana?" Kevin asked, surprised. "I've heard of her but never played her. Is she as good as they say she is?"

"She got invited, didn't she?" I pointed out.

"True."

"Okay—"

"Uh, how well do you know her? Is she also as beautiful as they say?"

"Very well and, yes, she is."

"I thought so. Proceed, please."

"Thank you. When we do steal the stuff, we're going to need a way to get off this island. I've got someone who may be able to arrange that for us, but first we've got to get a good look at the layout."

"You've scouted the outside already?" he asked.

"As well as I could. Stay with me on this one, Kevin, and there'll be plenty of cash in it for you."

"You said that," he reminded. "You certainly know the way to a man's loyalty, Nick."

"I know you, Kevin," I told him. "Tell me something. Why did you call Casey's room earlier today?"

He looked surprised.

"You've got the place wired, I see. I should have known. To tell you the truth, old man, I was quite taken with the young lady, but a man answered, so you know what I did."

"Sure," I said, "what any self-respecting gentleman would do, you hung up. Well, don't give up, Kevin. I think the lady would be susceptible to your particular brand of charm."

"Really? How good of you to say so, old chum. Uh, you and she don't have a little, uh, thing going, then?"

"Maybe just a little one," I admitted, "but that never

stopped you before, did it?"

"No, I suppose not. Ready for another drink?"

"Sure, why not. This time they're on you."

CHAPTER TWENTY-SEVEN

At a quarter to seven I went down to the dining room to meet Christine for dinner. She wasn't there yet, so I ambled out into the lobby just in time to see Casey crossing from the elevators to the front door.

She was dressed to the nines, tens, and beyond in a low-cut, no-back, split-up-the-sides gown. Just what the best-dressed newlywed bride wears to step out on her new husband.

A mile-long limo was waiting out front for her and a chauffeur, who looked suspiciously like another of Orantes's bodyguards, got out and opened the rear door for her. As she was getting into the car I could feel someone come up from behind me and peer over my shoulder. From the scent of her perfume, I knew that it was Christine.

"I'll bet you anything that she isn't going out to meet hubby," she said from behind me.

"Anything?" I asked, looking her in the eye.

"Even that," she affirmed confidently.

I sighed and said, "No bet. Ready for dinner?"

She nodded, saying, "I'm starved."

"Must be the excitement," I guessed and allowed her to precede me into the dining room.

We allowed the maitre d' to show us to a table and

ordered drinks. Christine looked smashing this time wearing an outfit that had long sleeves, but plunged down deeply in front showing off her ample breasts. The color enhanced her beauty—red—and the material clung to each seductive curve of her body. No woman could have worn that dress unless her figure matched Christine's. There simply weren't many bodies like hers. Her hair was down and hung past her shoulders, the way I like a woman's hair to be.

We chatted about what to have for dinner and didn't speak of other things until we had ordered.

She rested her chin on her hand when the waiter had gone off to see to our orders and said, "Who do you think she's going to meet, on this island, who could afford to send a car that looks like a houseboat on wheels to pick her up?"

"Who?"

"Who?" she repeated. "The little blond wifey, that's who. Who do you think?"

"Oh, her." I shrugged. "Damned if I know. Do you think she plays poker?"

She gave me a sly grin and said, "No, but I'll bet she just might be playing some other kind of game."

She kept looking at me as if she were waiting for me to let her in on some deep, dark secret, but I just shrugged again to indicate my ignorance in the matter.

"What do you suppose he'll do with her during the game tonight?" she asked.

"I don't know, Christine," I answered, trying not to sound too testy. I felt as if I was being interrogated—or tested. "Maybe you can tell me that when you get back tonight."

"Will you wait up for me?" she asked playfully.

At that point our dinner arrived, and we leaned back and ceased conversation until the waiter had served and left.

"Nick, have you given any thought to my offer of this morning?"

"Which offer?"

"About my helping you get what you want from Orantes's house," she reminded me, looking annoyed.

"I didn't admit that I wanted anything," I reminded her.

"No, you didn't admit it in so many words, but c'mon, Nick, I'm not dumb and neither are you, so let's stop fencing."

I looked at her across the table, for once wishing that I could take someone in my life at face value—but I couldn't, and that was the way of it. I couldn't afford that kind of a luxury, not if I wanted to stay alive a little longer—or keep her alive.

"Okay, Chris. Frankly, I have considered your offer, and I'm wondering why you would make such an offer without having any idea what you might be letting yourself in for." I leaned across the table and added, "You know, we really haven't known each other all that long."

"Don't you believe that I like you and only want to help you?" she asked.

"Now *you* c'mon, Christine. You're the one who said you wanted to stop playing games," I reminded her. "In my business, being skeptical is a way of life."

"And what business is that?"

"I've told you that already. I'm a private investigator."

"Yes, I know, but what is it you're into?"

"Answer my question first," I told her. "Why do you want to help me?"

She leaned back in her chair and put her fork down. She gave herself some time to think by taking a long, slow sip of her wine. As she drank with one hand, the fingers of the other tapped out a nervous tattoo on the table.

Finally, she made her decision and began to speak.

"Nick, I've been living a certain way for some time, now," she started her explanation. "Traveling where I want, when I want, never having to work, never really having to take anything seriously. Have you ever wondered what it would be like to live like that?"

I shook my head. The day I stopped taking everything seriously would be the day I cashed in my chips for good.

"It gets boring, Nick. Sometimes it can get very boring—and depressing. Don't get me wrong, I'm not saying I'd like to give it all up. On the whole, I like living this way, but every so often I would like to do something meaningful—or exciting."

That was the key word.

"I see."

"When I first met you I had the feeling that you were much more than you appeared to be. The experience on the float convinced me."

"Yeah," I agreed, "that was a convincer, all right."

"Did you think that being shot at frightened me?" she asked seriously.

"The thought had occurred to me," I admitted.

She shook her head.

"I was surprised at myself, Nick. I was excited by it, exhilarated, in fact. You've brought something new into my life." She leaned forward and added in a low voice, "You've brought me a feeling of danger, and it's like nothing I've ever felt before."

Very dramatic.

"I have to assume that your desire to get into Orantes's house has something to do with your—our—being shot at. If there's something there that you need, or want, then I might be in a position some time tonight to get it for you. I'd like to help, Nick, because it excites me. Is that what you wanted to hear?"

If I could have believed her, it would have been just what I wanted to hear. I would have liked very much to believe that she was just a rich lady out for some excitement and thrills, who had tired—however momentarily—of her easy life. What I had told her about my business wasn't true, but what I had said about being skeptical was. It was second nature to me, and it would take more than a couple of sweet nights together to change that.

"Okay, Christine."

"Does that mean you'll let me help? You believe me?" she asked eagerly.

"It means that I'll accept your explanation for now," I told her. "As far as tonight goes, just keep your eyes open while you're in the house."

"What am I looking for?"

"Just keep them open. You might see something you won't necessarily like."

"Like what?"

Like me.

"Never mind. Just keep your eyes open and remember what you see. We'll talk about you helping me afterward —if you still want to."

CHAPTER TWENTY-EIGHT

At eight fifteen I left Christine at her room to freshen up for her big night. Since I was being picked up fifteen minutes before she was, I went to my room to get ready and had to rush it, because I had another stop to make.

The stop was at the bridal suite, where I knocked heavily on the door. I anticipated that Trumball was inside with a set of earphones on, listening to Oswaldo Orantes's heavy breathing over that gown that Casey was wearing, and I wanted him to hear me knock the first time so I wouldn't have to do it again.

When he opened the door he was wearing a pair of headphones with the jack hanging loose. He made a face and asked, "What do you want?"

"Whatever it is, I'm not about to tell you about it from the hall. Can I come in?"

He scowled and stepped back impatiently to allow me to enter.

"I'm monitoring," he told me, showing his impatience.

"Has he scored yet?" I asked.

He scowled again and turned away from me to sit in front of his electronic equipment. He inserted the jack and began fiddling with the knobs.

The suite was opulent, to say the least. Just what

you'd expect from an outfit like Pleasure Island. The electronic equipment was set up on a writing desk which had obviously been moved into the room from elsewhere, probably the bedroom. It was set up in the center of the room.

"What do you do if she does get into trouble?" I asked him, waving my hand at the equipment.

"She's a big girl," he told me.

"Sure. Do you know how to work that thing?"

"Of course," he said without turning. "I've had adequate training with electronic equipment."

Yeah, I thought, about five minutes' worth, just before boarding the plane for the island.

"Okay, just listen up a second."

"Carter, I'm trying to run an operation here—" he began, but I cut him off.

"It's too late to let Casey know," I said loudly.

"Know what?" he asked.

"I've been invited by Orantes to play poker at his house this evening."

"What?" he shouted, standing up so quickly he knocked his chair over. "You can't go in there, Carter. You're backup. You should have cleared it with me—or Casey—"

"There wasn't any time. It's too late to tell her, so I'm telling you. I'm going in there to play cards. I won't take any action, but I'll keep a watch. How's she doing in there?"

"They're finishing dinner," he told me, picking up his chair and sitting in it again.

"All right. I should be out there by nine." I checked my watch; it was time to meet my car.

"Look, Carter, I don't know—"

"Trumball, dammit, I'm supposed to be a gambler as well as a professor. It's part of my cover. If I refuse this invitation, he's going to wonder why? Right?"

He tightened his lips, forced to agree with me against his will.

"You sit tight on your machine," I told him. "If she gets into a jam, at least I'll be there to help her out."

"You think he'll keep her around during the game?" he asked.

"It's possible, I don't know. We'll see when I get there."

Shaking his head he admitted, "It's not going quite the way we planned."

"Didn't expect him to be such a gentleman, huh?"

"He's just talking. He won't even show her around the house. It's as if—as if—"

As if he were just a little suspicious of her, maybe, I thought. Maybe he didn't want to show her too much. Or maybe that was what he did with all the blondes he brought up there. Just had dinner, and nothing more.

"I have to go—a car is picking me up. Listen, Trumball, we don't get along, I know that, but are we going to let that affect our work?"

He regarded me for a moment, then shook his head slowly.

"No, Carter. I don't like you, but I'm too much of a professional to let that interfere with business."

I kept myself from laughing and said, "Fine. I'll be seeing you."

"Carter—"

"What?"

"Keep any eye on her," he told me.

"Remember, Trumball, she's a big girl," I told him, and walked out.

CHAPTER TWENTY-NINE

I was the first to arrive, admitted by the bodyguard Orantes called José.

"Mr. Orantes is in the study. Follow me, please."

I followed him and found Orantes in the study alone. Casey was nowhere in sight.

"A drink, Mr. Collins?" he offered.

"Bourbon," I told him. José went to the bar and prepared my drink, and one for his boss.

"I'm first?" I asked.

"You are. The rest should be arriving shortly."

"All from the hotel?" I asked.

He waited a moment, watching me, then answered simply, "No," and offered no more.

"I would like to extend my compliments to your home. It's quite a place, and tastefully decorated. I don't mind admitting I'm somewhat of an interior design buff."

"Thank you. I've chosen much of what you see myself."

"Can I persuade you, then, into giving a private tour?"

"There are people coming here to play poker, Mr. Collins," he told me sternly.

"Oh, I'm sure there are others who would like to get

a tour of a beautiful house like this," I told him.

"Perhaps," he granted.

"I'll tell you what. Let's make a friendly wager."

"What kind of wager?" he asked, interested. Offer a gambler a bet, he'll get interested in a hurry.

"If someone else asks for a tour, then you'll grant one," I suggested.

"And if not?"

I patted my breast pocket, where I had an envelope filled with my winnings from the previous night.

"My entire winnings from last night," I offered.

"Which would still leave you with enough of a stake to play."

"For a while," I admitted. Like two hands, if I didn't take one of them.

He thought about it for a few moments, watching me the whole time. He was sitting in another—or the same —chair like the one he'd been seated in on the patio. They were probably the only kind of chairs he could be comfortable in. I'd bet he had one in each room.

"I'll take the bet, Mr. Collins, but with one condition," he told me.

"That being?"

"Mrs. Hall will not be included."

"You're a suspicious man, Mr. Orantes, but very well."

I approached him and we shook hands.

"We have a wager," he said.

I hoped Kevin wouldn't let me down, waiting for me to mention a possible tour of the house.

The next person to arrive was Christine, whose shock at seeing me there was very evident from the look on her face. I wondered if it was equally as evident to Orantes.

"I believe you know each other," Orantes said, not rising for Christine as he had failed to rise for me.

"Yes, we do. Hello, Christine."

"Nick," she said, recovering nicely from her initial shock.

Orantes offered her a drink, and by the time José had it ready Kevin had arrived. Orantes introduced him to Christine and me as Joseph James.

"This is a great pleasure for me," Kevin told Christine after he'd kissed her hand. "I've heard a lot about you, Mrs. Hall, and I'm looking forward to playing against you."

"I'm flattered."

Kevin looked at me and I tried to pass him a message with my eyes. For a moment I thought he was going to fail me, but he was right on cue.

"This is quite a place you have here, Mr. Orantes. Would it be imposing to ask you to possibly—"

"Of course," Orantes said, casting a blank glance my way, revealing neither surprise nor suspicion, even though I knew he was feeling at least one of them. "I'll conduct a tour myself before we sit down to play."

"Splendid," Kevin said, rubbing his palms together. "Thank you."

There were to be three other players, and they all arrived within moments of each other. I wondered how many had arrived by sea.

Orantes introduced each of the remaining three as they arrived.

Jock Owens was from Texas. He looked it and acted it. He was a tall, thin man with incredibly large hands and long fingers. He held his white stetson in those two hands and with exaggerated Texas charm introduced himself to Christine. He was too good to be true—or was that my overactive skepticism at work again?

John Woodley Farrel was from California. And he was what you might call a bit of a fop. He was about five-six, thin, with long brown hair that curled up over his collar. When offered a drink he requested anisette but settled for sherry.

Kasimir Parlov was either Russian or Czeck. He was nearly as big as Orantes, but he was all muscle. He had massive shoulders and arms but not a hint of a belly. His hair was gray and short-cropped, and he had no neck to speak of. His hands were thick-fingered, and I couldn't imagine them holding a playing card without mangling it.

When Orantes announced that there would be a short tour of the house before the game started, the last three men exhibited impatience, but I caught Christine's eye and, bless her, she went along.

"That's a lovely idea," she remarked, so the others tagged along with us as Orantes took us from room to room, hitting all of them but one.

The room he didn't take us to was on the second floor. We passed the same door going up and coming down, and Orantes never made mention of it. I didn't, either. I didn't have to. I knew that was the room. The only thing I was worried about was whether Casey and the papers were in that room and if she was making the switch right now. But then I realized that would not be the case. Orantes wouldn't leave Casey or anyone else alone in that room with the papers.

That meant Casey had to be somewhere else, and the only other room we hadn't seen yet was the room we were going to play in.

He lead us back downstairs and into a large room with a green felt-topped table in the center of it. There were two unopened decks of cards and a turret-wheel of different color poker chips. Behind the bar stood Casey, and the look on her face told me she wasn't happy. Things had obviously not gone the way she had expected. I assumed by her presence that Orantes had asked—or instructed—her to be the hostess for the game. She wouldn't like that, but she'd go along with it.

She barely hid her surprise when she saw me among the people being ushered into the room.

"This is where we will play," Orantes was finishing as we entered. "The lady behind the bar is our hostess, Casey."

Obviously, what Orantes had in mind for all those blonde ladies included not only dinner, but acting as hostess for his gambling parties. If there were any further plans, they remained to be seen.

I also noticed the presence of José, one of his bodyguards, who was standing in a corner with his hands folded in front of him. He wouldn't move for the duration of the game.

"Please, take seats around the table," Orantes instructed. His place was made obvious by the presence of one of those oversize armchairs. When Kasimir Parlov expressed distaste with his chair, Orantes instructed one of his bodyguards to bring a large armchair like his from one of the other rooms. When he tried it, Parlov thanked Orantes, who said it was nothing. He wanted everyone to be comfortable while he was taking their money. Everyone laughed.

We all gave our drink orders to Casey, who prepared them and then served them. Our eyes met and locked as she set mine down, and I could feel the ice emanating from them, along with the question, what the hell was I doing there? I smiled at her and thanked her.

When we all had our drinks, Orantes cracked a deck and began to deal the first hand. For once Christine was not directly opposite me, but one seat to the left. Kevin was opposite me and, consequently, was seated right next to Christine. Orantes was two players to my right.

From where I sat I had a clear view of the entrance to the room. I could also see the stairway beyond, which led to the second floor. The door that we had passed going up and coming down was on the landing between the first and second floors. I turned my head and saw José, still holding his position. From where Orantes sat I was sure he couldn't see out the door to the stairway, but José would be able to.

After five hands, I asked Orantes for the men's room. He told me it was outside and to the left. If I were to walk straight to the stairway instead of to the bathroom, José would see me. That meant I couldn't very well claim I was looking for the men's room and got lost. José didn't look like the type who would buy that.

I wouldn't buy it, either.

Kevin got hot early and was way ahead after the first hour. Orantes and Christine looked like they were holding even. Everyone else was losing, but J.W. Farrel was the biggest loser of all. You could tell because he was letting us know.

"Haven't had a run of bad luck like this in months," he complained. He chain-smoked lavender-smelling cigarettes and kept mopping his brow with a yellow silk hanky.

When he complained, Tex Owens always answered him the same way. "Shaddup!"

That was just the first hour, however. After that there was very little talk at all, except for "raise," "call," and "fold."

It was two hours before the first really interesting hand developed. It was between myself, Orantes, and J.W. Farrel.

We were five cards into a hand of seven card stud. Farrel was head man on board with a pair of jacks, and he had forced everyone out but Orantes and myself. The big man had a pair of tens showing, but I had him pegged for trips. I had a pair of sixes in the hole, and one more on board.

Farrel was doing the betting, Orantes was raising, and I was playing coy and just calling. I had three sixes, but I also had three clubs on the table. They must have thought I was nuts, going for a flush. I knew that if I pulled another pair, I had Orantes's three tens beat—unless he pulled another pair. Farrel had two pair, I felt sure of that. The only way he could win was to pull a third jack—only I knew that Christine had folded a jack, which gave him only one chance to be King of the Hand.

I had one of Orantes's tens—the club—on the table in front of me, so the strongest he could be was tens full.

The deal belonged to Tex, and he gave us our sixth cards.

Farrel pulled a five, giving him two pair on the table.

Orantes's card was a three, no help. I still had him pegged for a third ten in the hole, with his fourth one sitting in front of me. My sixes on board were joined by a little deuce. That little deuce matched the little deuce I had in the hole, with my third six.

I had my full house.

Farrel opened the betting with a thousand. Orantes raised him a thousand. I tested the water by raising, but only five hundred.

Farrel looked at me, then at my sixes. I felt that if he had his full house, he'd raise, and if he didn't, he'd just call. He called both raises. Orantes called me and raised me five hundred. I called, and so did Farrel—which is what they mean by throwing good money after bad.

Tex dealt the last card.

Mine was a jack, which meant that Farrel couldn't win the hand. The best he could have had, with another five in the hole, was fives full, and that wasn't good enough.

Farrel had been playing for that jack, and knowing that he hadn't pulled it enabled me to notice the slight look of disappointment on his face when he looked at his last card. He was finished.

Now I only had to worry about Orantes. I had one advantage over him. I knew that Farrel's hand was dead; he didn't. He was still playing against two of us. I was only playing against one man.

Farrel opened the betting. He wanted us to think he'd made his jacks full, or he would have checked.

Orantes bet a thousand. He wanted us to think he had his tens full, and that he didn't believe Farrel.

I raised a thousand. I had to. I knew I had Farrel beat, and I'd never forgive myself if I didn't see Orantes through to the end.

And if I didn't beat him, maybe I'd throw a scare into him.

If the man was scared, however, he sure didn't show it. He bumped me another thousand without hesitating. In between my raise and his raise, Farrel decided that one of us had to have him beat, so he bowed out. I had been hoping that his hand might occupy some of Orantes's time, but the big man was too good for that. He knew he had Farrel beat before the foppish little man folded. He may not have had a better hand than J.W., but he had the man beat.

Thoughts raced through my mind very rapidly. I didn't want to seem as if I were hesitating. The only problem I had was raising without hesitation, or just calling and saving myself some money. I decided to call, cut my losses, and wait for the next hand.

"I call."

"Two pair," Orantes called, showing tens and, in the hole, a pair of eights.

"Damn!" J.W. Farrel exploded. His jacks over had Orantes's hand beat.

But not mine.

"Sixes full," I called, and raked in my substantial winnings.

"Hoo, Lord!" J.W. exclaimed, now that he knew that he would have been second best, at best. Orantes threw him a look I interpreted as disgust. His face didn't change, but I thought I detected a slight difference around the mouth.

"Next hand, gents," Tex said, passing the remainder of the deck to the next dealer, Christine. She managed to throw me a little high sign with her eyes, which meant she forgave me for not telling her I was going to be at the game.

I caught Kevin's eye at one point in the evening and managed to convey the message that I wanted him to go to the men's room. I wanted him to take a look at the hall and whatever else he could see while he was out there. We'd compare notes later.

I could have kissed Christine for what she did after Kevin had returned. Without any visual prompting from me—although I had been trying to think of a way to plant the idea in her head—she asked Orantes where she could go to "freshen up."

The next big hand developed among myself, Tex, and Kevin. I noticed Orantes watching me closely, looking for telltale signs, a giveaway, something he could use the next time we tangled in the same big hand.

I kept my face straight, which was hard, because by the time the seven cards were dealt, I had the kind of hand gamblers dream about and want to sing about when they get it.

I had a hidden hand.

My table cards read this way: six of hearts, five of hearts, jack of clubs and ace of clubs. In the hole I had the ten, queen, and king of clubs. Kevin and Tex had to be figuring me for a medium straight, and I knew Tex had me beat. He had four diamonds showing, and he bought the fifth on the last card. I knew because his upper lip developed a sheen whenever he had a good hand, and after the seventh card, he was "sheening" up a storm. He had to have the money to keep on being a professional gambler, because with a giveaway like that he wasn't even going to make money playing cards.

Kevin was taking what I said about working together —"possibly" working together—to heart. He was building me a pot because he couldn't possibly have anything better than two pair. Orantes had dismissed Kevin, however, as a serious card player, and he was watching me. He missed—at least, I hoped he missed—the fact that Kevin was betting into me and building the pot up. Tex was too intent on his own cards to notice anything else.

Finally, Kevin had to fold or become obvious. When he did, and Tex finally called my raise without raising me back—I think I just outlasted him, he was so eager to show his hand—I turned over my cards and watched the tall Texan go white.

"Damn!"

Damn was right, because from the look on Kasimir Parlov's face, Kevin's shenanigans hadn't escaped him. If Parlov chose to talk to our host about it, we could have been in serious trouble.

Luckily, Kevin noticed Parlov eyeing him, and the next time he could have worked his stuff, he chose not to. That seemed to satisfy Parlov.

By the time the night was over, I was wondering how Kevin, J.W., and Tex had wangled invitations from Orantes. None of the three of them had what it took to be professional gamblers. Tex had that giveaway, J.W. was too emotional, and Kevin was too undisciplined.

"Gentlemen—and lady—thank you for a most interesting evening. If any of you are interested in another game, I'd like you all to stay on at the hotel as my guests, and return here Tuesday evening," Orantes announced at the end of the game.

"What's wrong with tomorrow night?" Tex asked.

"I have another engagement tomorrow evening," Orantes told him and everyone else, but that's all he'd say.

I was surprised when Orantes pulled me aside and asked, "Have you any objection to sharing a car back to the hotel?"

"With whom?"

"Mrs. Hall?"

"No, I don't have any objections at all."

We went back in two cars; Christine and I in one, and the rest of the players in the other. That was just as well. I'd ask Kevin what they talked about during the drive.

When I got into the back seat of Orantes's limo, Christine was already there.

"Well, fancy meeting you here," she remarked.

"I can explain."

"Fine, I'd like to hear an explanation," she told me. "Your room or mine?"

"Let's make it yours," I told her, thinking about Casey. "We're less likely to be interrupted."

When the phone first rang in Christine's room, we were not inclined to answer it. We both had our minds on other things.

The second time it rang, I told Christine not to answer it.

"Why not? Do you know who it is?" she asked.

"Probably some friends of mine, trying to locate me," I told her. "I don't want to be located right now."

The caller had to be Casey, wanting an explanation about last night—more of an explanation than I had given Trumball. I wondered when she had gotten back to the hotel from the big house. She hadn't left with the rest of us. Had Orantes had something else in mind for her, after the game?

She'd get her answers and I'd get mine, but that would

be tomorrow—or rather, later in the day, since it was nearly four A.M.

Christine and I were lying in her bed, and she said that she thought it was about time for that explanation.

"If you think I deserve one, that is," she added.

"I just didn't want anyone to know in advance that I'd be there," I told her. I tried to change the subject by saying, "Besides, after that trip to the ladies' room, why wouldn't you deserve an explanation?"

She laughed.

"I kept my eyes open, too. Did you see where the ladies' room was?"

"I sure did." I had watched her when she left. The ladies' room was upstairs, and she must have gone past that locked door to get to it.

"It was still locked," she said as if reading my mind.

"What was?"

"That door to the room Orantes wouldn't show us."

"You tried it?" She nodded. "That was foolish, Chris. You could have gotten caught."

"Nick, I told you I wanted to help you. Standing outside that door, trying the knob, was very exciting."

"Getting caught wouldn't have been," I told her.

"Tell me about it."

"I'll tell you about it, all right," I told her, sounding like I was coming from an old Cagney movie. "You want to help me?"

"Yes."

"Then you do as I say, no more and no less, okay?"

"Okay," she agreed, her eyes shining with excitement.

"You, I, and one other party are going to get together sometime today and put together everything we saw last night in that house. Among the three of us, we should be able to come up with a pretty good picture of what the inside of that house looks like. At least, the part that we're interested in."

"The area around that locked door," she said, just to show that she was staying with me.

"Yes. You were right, Chris. There is something in that house I want, and it's got to be behind that door."

"That's why he wouldn't show the room to us during the tour. He didn't want anyone to see the inside of it."

"Right."

"Who else is involved, Nick?" she asked. "The little blond bride?"

"She's involved, but not in the way you think."

Right then the phone rang again.

"Don't answer it," I told her. "Let's get some sleep. We've got some planning to do tomorrow."

She giggled like a schoolgirl and said. "Sounds to me like you're planning a robbery or something."

Now she thought I was a master criminal, and that seemed to excite her even more.

So much so that we didn't get to sleep until much later than I had intended.

CHAPTER THIRTY

I knew I couldn't avoid a confrontation with Casey, whose dander was bound to be sky-high. The phone had rung every half hour in Christine's room until six o'clock, which didn't make it very easy to sleep—or to do anything else. At six, it finally stopped, and I fell asleep and slept until nine. I left Christine asleep, and was back in my room by nine fifteen. After a shower I called Casey's room.

"Yeah, hello?" her voice came on, sounding as if she'd been awakened by the phone.

Good. I hoped she had.

"Hi, how about some breakfast, Mrs. Tremayne?"

"You! Where are you? Where the hell have you been?" she demanded.

"I'll tell you over breakfast."

"Allan's in the shower. I'll wait until he's—"

"After last night, Mrs. Tremayne, I don't think anyone is going to be too surprised to see you having breakfast with me without the mister. You weren't exactly inconspicuous leaving the hotel last night, you know."

There was a moment of silence, during which I could hear her breathing, then she said, "Well, all right then. I'll meet you on the veranda in fifteen minutes, Nick. I want to hear your explanation for last night, and I hope it's a good one."

Once again I made sure I was first for my appointment with her. I had two Bloody Mary's waiting when she arrived, attracting the eyes of the early-morning male bathers.

She was wearing a short, powder blue jumpsuit that showed plenty of her athletic-looking thighs and calves. It was open at the neck, revealing the swell of her breasts. The only thing that kept her from looking like a contented beach blonde was the anger that showed in her eyes and in the firm set of her jaw.

When she sat down across from me she ignored the drink in front of her and proceeded to tear into me.

"What the hell did you think you were doing, showing up at Orantes's house last night?" she challenged.

"I was invited. Didn't Allan tell you? I reported to him, as agent-in-charge, the reason I was accepting Orantes's invitation."

"Well now, as agent-in-charge, I want to hear your explanation. And it better—"

I leaned forward and told her tightly, "Don't say it, Casey. I'll give you an explanation, not that I think you deserve one. Just keep your mouth shut long enough to listen."

She looked like she was going to talk back, but she caught herself and settled back to listen, arms crossed beneath her breasts.

"For one thing, I didn't get the invitation until very late last night, after you had left the hotel. I got to Allan as soon as I could to let him know. The reason I gave him for accepting—so as not to arouse suspicion—was true, as far as it went. The other reason was you."

"Me?"

"Yes. I was worried about you," I told her, being careful not to lay it on too thick. She was an agent, but she was also a woman, and there are certain things that women are susceptible to. I was banking on that to make Casey believe my story—for a while, anyway, until the agent in her took over.

Her face softened just a bit, and I knew I had her hooked.

"I didn't like the idea of you going into that house alone, Casey, you know that. When the invitation came, I saw it as a chance to go in and . . . back you up. How did it go, last night? Did you get the notes?"

She shook her head, and her expression became one of puzzlement.

"I can't understand it, Nick. Orantes was very attentive, very gentlemanly. He never left me alone for a minute, and yet he never laid a hand on me. He left me in the cardroom with José while he greeted all of the players. Then, after you all left, he brought me into his den for a nightcap, and had me driven home."

"Where's his den?"

"Well, he showed it to you. It's on the first floor, farther down the hall from the cardroom."

"Oh, that's right."

She looked at me for a long moment, then said, "You noticed it too, didn't you?"

"Noticed what?"

"That locked door, on the landing between the first and second floors. He wouldn't let me even get near the door. He either stayed with me or had someone with me the whole time I was there."

"Maybe he's just naturally suspicious," I offered. "We passed that door twice—once on the way up and once on the way down—and he never even made mention of it. That must be where he's keeping the notes."

"Maybe that's also where he's intending to hold the auction," she suggested. "We've got to get into that house again."

"Did he say anything about having you back?" I asked.

"He said he'd call me. He thanked me for acting as his hostess, and said that if I were going to be on the island for another week or more, that he might have another game and would call to see if I would like to come back."

"What did you say?"

She made a face and answered, "I told him I'd be delighted."

I laughed.

"I thought you were great as a hostess," I told her. "As a bartender, you could use some practice, but overall I think you did a marvelous job."

"Oh, shut up," she said, but she couldn't keep herself from smiling when she said it. All the anger she'd arrived with was gone.

"Could we get together tonight?" she asked.

"How would that look?"

"You're the one who said that no one would be surprised by anything I did from now on. Why don't we give them a treat?"

"Will you report back to the colonel, now that your first plan didn't work?" I asked.

"Allan is doing that now," she told me. "And my plan wasn't a complete failure, Nick. I did get into the house," she reminded me.

"Yes, but so did I—and I'm not even a blonde."

"Neither is your girlfriend, and she got in, too. She's very pretty, isn't she—if you like older women."

"She's a very good player," I remarked.

"I'll bet."

"I guess you and Allan will come up with a new plan pretty soon."

"We're working on it. I'll keep you informed. In the future, Nick, I think you had better just stay in the background. I appreciate your concern, I really do, but stay in the background. We'll make use of you, I promise."

She leaned forward and covered my hand with hers. I smiled and told her, "You're the boss."

She took a sip from her Bloody Mary and then said, "I have to get back. I want to find out what the colonel's reaction to Allan's report was. Call me later?"

"I will," I promised.

She patted my hand, saying, "You're a very sweet man, Nick."

"You're okay too."

She got up and trotted up the steps, back into the hotel. All the male eyes—including mine—watched her firm little rump disappear inside, appreciating the athletic grace with which she moved.

Considering their first plan, I was afraid to find out what they'd come up with next.

I was going to have to firm up my own plans and put them into action soon, which meant getting together with Kevin and Christine, first separately, then together.

I'd get the papers we were there to get, and apologize later to Casey, her colonel, and Hawk for the way I went about it, but I was going to do it the way I always did things.

My way.

CHAPTER THIRTY-ONE

My next stop of the day was to talk to Al Nuss.

"Is Al Nuss around?" I asked the desk clerk.

"He's off duty, sir," he informed me.

"It's very important that I speak with him. Can you tell me where his room is?"

"Sure. Take the elevator down one floor and turn right when you get out. It's room A-fourteen."

"Thanks," I said, passing him a five dollar bill.

"Thank you, sir."

Nuss answered the door clad in a silk bathrobe.

"Well, you certainly didn't buy that on a bellboy's salary, did you?"

"Just something I picked up . . . along the way," he told me, looking down at himself. "What can I do for you?"

"Can I come in? I'd like to talk to you about something," I told him.

"Sure."

He backed up to allow me to enter.

"A drink?" he offered.

I was looking at the furniture in the room, which obviously was not hotel furniture. When I turned he had opened an expensive-looking cellarette, revealing an impressive array of liquor bottles and glasses.

"I'll say this for you, Al. You live pretty well."

"I make do, Nick. Something?" he asked, pointing to the bottles.

"Uh, no, thanks, not right now. Can we talk?"

"Sure. It's your nickel."

It was adding up to considerably more than that, and would probably get even more expensive before we finished talking.

He sat down on the couch and I sat opposite him.

"Al, I'm going to need transportation off the island," I explained.

"That's no problem. There are shuttles four times a day. Just let the hotel know—"

"No, I'm not talking about shuttles, Al. I'm talking about . . . unscheduled transportation."

He regarded me in silence for a moment, then said. "I think I see."

"Do you?"

"Yeah, I think I do, but why don't you clear it up for me, Nick," he said, leaning forward. "I mean, why don't you clear it all up?"

I'd told him two different stories already, but he seemed prepared to accept a third one.

"Okay, Al. Straight stuff."

He smiled. "Sure."

I frowned at him, but he continued to smile inanely at me.

"I'm going to rip Orantes off," I told him straight out.

His eyebrows went up in surprise, and he leaned back as if to take a long, relaxed, new look at me.

"I don't believe it," he finally said.

"It's true," I told him, then added quite truthfully, "truer than anything else I've told you."

He squinted at me and asked, "You're serious, aren't you?"

"Very."

"Damn, you are, aren't you?" He got up and walked around the couch once. "You're gonna rip the big man off. Do you know who you're dealing with?"

"I know, but it's got to be done, Al—and I need your help," I added.

"Transportation off the island after the job?"

"Right. After I'm done, I don't want to have to come back to the hotel, or even stay on the island longer than is absolutely necessary."

"Are you alone in this?"

"For now. I'm thinking about drafting a couple of recruits."

"Somebody in mind?"

"Yeah," I said, nodding, "I've got a couple of people in mind."

He sat down on the couch.

"Do you need someone with experience?" he asked.

"You mean, you?"

"Yeah."

"You've had experience in this area? In New York?"

"New York, L.A., Chicago . . . you name the place, I've been there and I've left my mark behind."

"Anybody looking for you as a result?" I asked.

"Nah, I'm free and clear. You wouldn't have to worry about that if you take me on."

"Can you get me transportation off the island?"

"I can get you a chopper," he said confidently.

"If I tell you when, can you have it by the dock at the base of the cliff by Orantes's house?"

"No sweat. Do I get cut in?"

"Will that settle our account?"

"I don't know what you're after, but if it's coming

from Orantes, it must be worth plenty, so yeah, that'll settle our account."

"Okay, Al, you're in."

"How many in on the job?"

"With you there's four. I'll be talking with the others today."

"When do you think we'll go?"

"I'm not sure, but sometime within the next two days would be a safe bet," I told him.

"I'll be ready. I'll, uh, have to bring in a pilot. How much can we go for?"

It was "we" already. He didn't waste any time getting into the spirit of things.

"Get him for whatever you can. I'll leave that up to you," I told him.

"How many people will be going in the chopper?" he asked.

"Well, if we keep your involvement quiet, you can always come back here afterward."

Kevin would want to get off the island—of that I was certain—so he and I would be going for sure. Depending on how involved Christine got in the operation, she could either stay or go. I still didn't know myself if Casey and Trumball would end up involved, too. That meant that would be as many as five people in the chopper, or as few as two. That's what I told him.

"Okay."

I got up to leave, and he walked me to the door.

"I'll keep in touch, Al, and let you know when I'm sure of what we're going to do. I still have to talk to the others. We'll have a final briefing when I have everyone together."

"The others can still back out?" he asked.

'It's a possibility," I admitted.

He shrugged and said, "Bigger split for us."

"Sure. I'll be in touch."

I hoped he wouldn't be too disappointed when he found out that his split might amount to a simple "thank you" from his country.

CHAPTER THIRTY-TWO

I found Kevin in his room enjoying a late breakfast. He answered the door with a big napkin on his neck and chewing a mouthful of eggs.

"I knew it," I told him.

"Knew what?"

"Beneath all that wit and charm beats the heart of a real slob," I told him.

"Yes, well, everyone has to let their hair down sometimes, old man. Would you like to come in?"

"I'd love it."

Inside he asked, "How about a cup of coffee?"

"If you can spare it."

"I had two pots sent up, Nicholas. I was expecting you," he said with a wide smile.

He sat at his breakfast tray, and I took my cup of coffee and settled on the couch.

It was funny. Kevin and I had worked together once or twice before, when the situation dictated it, but for the most part we had spent our careers as adversaries. Yet, out of everyone on this island, he was the one I trusted the most. Part of the reason for that was the fact that I knew that Kevin was not the Specialist.

Two years before we had been together in Switzerland while the Specialist was taking care of victim number fourteen in Australia. We had heard about it at the same time and had a long discussion about who we thought the Specialist might be.

He said that, on occasion, he had thought it might be me.

I told him that the thought that it might have been him had never entered my mind.

There was one other occasion when I knew where Kevin was during one of the Specialist's hits, so I was positive that it wasn't him.

"Okay, Kevin, let's level."

"I thought we had been. I'm here about the notes Orantes is auctioning; you're here to steal them, right?"

"Right, but there's something else."

"What?"

I took the note informing me that I was the next victim from my pocket and handed it to him.

"We have a friend in town."

He read the note, then passed it back.

"Has he made a pass?"

"In a way."

He frowned and asked, "In what way?"

"He's shot at me twice—"

"And missed?" he asked, surprised.

"Well, he's missed deliberately. I'm sure he could have had me cold either time."

"That's not his usual play," he said, shaking his head. "He doesn't normally play games."

"I know, that's what puzzles me, but I've been working under a handicap all this time."

"Watching for him."

"Right."

"What about your injury?"

I flexed my foot experimentally, and it felt pretty good.

"It feels okay. I haven't been using my cane, but then

I haven't been in a position to test it yet, why?"

"Well, Nicholas, if you want me to back you, I want to be sure that you're in shape to do the same for me . . . if the situation should warrant it, you know what I mean?"

"I'll back you, Kevin, don't worry about that," I assured him.

"What about your partners?" he asked.

"Kevin, right now you're the only person on this island I trust completely," I told him.

"Nicholas, I am touched, I truly am."

"Just don't disappoint me."

"Have I ever?" he asked innocently.

"Well, there was that time in Mexico, when I was supposed to meet this señorita—"

"Okay, okay, never mind. More coffee?"

I accepted a second cup.

"What's the plan?" he asked.

"So far there's three of us—"

"Who's the third, if I'm the only one you can trust?"

"There's a bellboy in the hotel who's probably using this place and the job to hide out from the law in the States. He's got a racket going, and can supply us with everything from guns to a helicopter."

"Will that be our escape route?"

"Yours and mine, yeah."

"What about the others?"

"If they need it. If we can get through this thing without revealing that they're involved, they can go back to the hotel and leave by conventional shuttle. My bellboy can have our chopper ready any time I say."

"That's some bellboy."

"He's from New York, but he's done some time in L.A. and Chicago, pulling petty thievery mostly, I think. He lucked into something here, some kind of contact who gets him anything he needs."

"What does he charge?" Kevin asked, ever mindful of money matters.

"We're cutting him in for a piece of the action."

"A piece of what action?" he asked.

I shrugged.

"He thinks we're after something that's worth a lot of money," I explained.

"We are."

"Not to him."

He shook his head, grinning happily, and said, "To me."

"Kevin, have you ever done anything just out of friendship?"

"Once."

"What happened?"

"My friend shot me and stole my money."

"Oh."

"Then he stole my girl."

"Okay, forget it."

"Speaking of girls, that Christine plays a mean game of poker, doesn't she?" he asked.

"Speaking of poker, how'd you do?"

"Ah, I held my own," he said evasively.

"How much did you lose?"

"A couple of thousand."

"You're lucky you play so tight. Oh, yeah, one other thing."

"What?"

"Don't try and build me any pots. Let's not advertise the fact that we're working together, okay?"

"Fine."

He finished his breakfast and pushed the tray away.

"Shall we go over what we both saw?" he asked.

"Not yet. I want to get us all together so we don't have to go over any of it twice. I have one other person to talk to this morning, then I'll call you and let you know when we'll meet."

"As you wish. I think I'll take a shower now and then check out some of the female population on this island. Have you any objection to my calling Mrs. Hall?"

I shook my head.

"None at all. Be my guest."

"That's very kind of you Nicholas. I will wait for your call."

"If you're not in, I'll leave a message at the desk. Check with them every hour or so."

"I will," he promised.

I left him to his shower. As long as he thought there was plenty of money in this for him, I could count on him.

All I had to do was figure out a way for him to make plenty of money.

CHAPTER THIRTY-THREE

The team now consisted of myself, Kevin, and Al Nuss. I knew Christine wanted to be a part of it, but I wanted to give her one more chance to change her mind. I wanted to make her aware of the danger she could be in.

When I knocked on her door she answered wearing a negligee, looking as if she had just gotten out of bed.

"Sleeping late, I see."

"Well, last night was a very tiring night," she said, and I knew she wasn't talking about poker.

"Why don't we send down for some coffee?" I suggested, shutting the door behind me.

"Why don't you do that while I shower?" she asked.

"Okay. Don't be too long."

She decided to tease me and dropped the negligee just before entering the bedroom. I got a flash of tan and white buttocks before she disappeared from sight. I picked up her negligee and dropped it on a chair, then called room service and told them to send up a pot of coffee and a couple of cups.

She came out of the shower with her hair up in a towel and her body wrapped in a short, terry cloth robe. She was still wet, and the robe showed every contour of her body.

"You've got to be the sexiest thing I've ever seen in the morning," I told her.

"It's afternoon, dear."

"That, too."

She came over to me, and I gathered her up into my arms. Her body was damp and full, her mouth was warm and alive, and I was getting hot and bothered.

"I want to talk to you, Christine," I told her.

"I don't want to talk," she said, kissing me again.

"It's important," I insisted, and sat her down on the couch.

"All right, go ahead and talk. I'll keep my distance," she promised, backing away a whole inch, folding her hands primly in her lap.

"I want you to understand what you might be getting yourself into," I told her.

"Oh, Nick, not that again. I want to do this, darling, don't you understand? Not only for you, but for me. Please, please, let me help and stop trying to talk—or scare—me out of it. All right?"

Shaking my head I said, "Okay, have it your way."

She closed up the inch she had previously backed up, and her mouth was on mine again. She tasted so clean and smelled so fresh, but before we could really get started, the coffee arrived.

"I'll get dressed," she told me, "and you answer the door."

"Okay."

I let the bellboy in with the tray, and he wheeled it over in front of the couch.

"Thank you," I told him, handing him a dollar.

"You have to sign for it, sir," he said.

"Okay."

The fact that I've spent an awful lot of my time in hotels actually saved my life. Bellboys, when they deliver food to your room, usually have the check either in their hand or on the tray. This particular bellboy reached into his pocket for the check, which struck me as odd, so I watched his hand as he dipped into his pocket—ostensibly for the check—and came out with a knife.

He used one motion which, had I not been tipped off, would have found me skewered and on the floor. His hand came out and he slashed at my midsection, but I was able to jump back and avoid it, upsetting the tray as I did. The coffee went flying onto the couch and the floor, and he kicked at the tray to get it out of the way so he could come at me again.

At this point, Christine came running out of the bedroom to find out what was going on. Still clad in her robe, which had fallen open, her hands flew to her mouth as she realized what was happening.

My assailant slashed at me again, and I grabbed up a cushion from the couch to use as a shield. He was holding the knife low, in a forward grip, which showed he was a pro. Again he slashed at me and put a good-sized rip in my pillow. The stuffing began to fly out, reducing its effectiveness as a shield. It was time for me to get offensive, or get poked.

I threw what was left of the pillow at his face, and when he flinched I threw a kick at his knife hand.

In the back of my mind I was thinking, kick with the bad foot, put the weight on the good one. The bad foot made contact with his knife hand and took it quite well. Unfortunately, so did his hand; he didn't drop the knife, further evidence that I was up against a pro.

Was he the Specialist?

As we circled each other I took a good look at him. He was tall, with dark hair and an ugly face which seemed to be comprised of lumps and angles. His nose was a lump, his chin was an angle, there were lumps above each eye, his mouth was an angle. He was about thirty-five or forty and thin. He didn't seem to be physically strong, and if I could get inside the knife without losing a limb, I thought I could take him out.

The problem was getting inside.

When I feinted in, he jumped back. When I moved back, he came forward. It was getting monotonous, and in its first real test, my bad foot was getting tired. If we kept it up much longer, the foot was going to get to be a liability. There was no pain, it just began to feel increasingly weaker.

We'd moved around the couch toward the center of the room. I kept backing up now, trying to get him used to moving forward. When I got back to the window he was so used to moving forward that when I moved in, he kept coming. It was his first mistake—and his last. The knife went over my head as I came in low. I got my arms around his knees and lifted him up and over. He went flying off his feet, over my head, through and out the window. All of the broken glass went out with him, but we were so far up I didn't hear him or it hit the ground.

They did, though. It was like snow. You didn't have to see it fall to know that it did.

Christine walked over to me slowly, then to the window, but she didn't look out. Instead she turned to me, "He's dead."

"That'd be a good guess," I told her.

Her eyes were like saucers, and if she was acting she was doing a damn good job of it.

I walked up to her and stood inches away.

"Does this bring it home, Christine? What I've been trying to tell you? Does this show you what you might be getting yourself in for?"

She remained quiet for a few seconds, then firmed up her chin and said, "I want to help."

"Enough to take the heat on this yourself?"

"What do you mean?"

"When they figure out what room he dove out of,

they'll be coming up here. Probably a house detective, or security chief, with the manager. They'll want to know what happened, and I don't want to get caught up in an inquiry. They'll hold me until they can get some representative of the law down here. That will put a crimp in what I have to do, Christine. Do you understand?"

She nodded.

"Yes."

"When they ask you what happened, what will you tell them?" I asked.

"I ordered breakfast—"

"Why two cups?"

"I was expecting company."

"Who?"

"A friend."

"Who?"

"None of your business," she shouted.

I nodded, then asked, "A man?"

"Yes."

"Did he show up?"

"No."

"What happened after you ordered breakfast?"

"The bellboy delivered it. I let him in. I was wearing" —she paused and looked down at herself—"I was wearing this robe and he started talking about how good I looked. He asked me if I'd like to tip him in the bedroom. When I asked him to leave—"

"Good girl," I told her, butting her off before she could run through the whole spiel. She'd do all right.

"I'll be in my room," I told her. "Call me when they leave."

"They won't hold me?"

I shook my head.

"Not the way you looked when you told me that story, honey. Just don't be so brave about it, you know? Cry a little, that always works."

She smiled a small, wan smile and said, "Okay, Nick."

"You still want to help?"

"Yes," she said without hesitation.

"All right. We're going to meet with a couple of other people who are going to help. When you call me, I'll tell you where and when."

"All right."

I took her gently by the shoulders and kissed her. "You okay?"

"I'm fine. What about you? Are you—"

"No, I'm not hurt. I've got to go, Chris. There should be a crowd gathering below by now. They'll be up here soon."

"I'll be ready."

"I know you will. You'll be great."

I left her standing in front of the broken window, shoulders hunched as if she were cold. I knew that as soon as I left she would look out the window.

CHAPTER THIRTY-FOUR

I had my team: Kevin, Al Nuss, and Christine. If I felt better about Casey, I'd use her. She had spent more time in the house than any of us. If I thought I could use her without having to take Trumball as well, I might have gone ahead. I didn't think I could. I didn't think he'd let me.

Hell, I didn't think she'd let me.

For better or for worse—for want of a better phrase— they were partners. She had him programmed to work the way she wanted, and he went along with it because . . . well, probably because he loved her, which was the wrong reason in this business.

Still, she had seen more than we had inside that house. Her information could be invaluable.

I'd try it without her, and use her only as a last resort.

I went back to my room to figure out where and when to get everyone together. The where was easy. Christine and I had been seen together much more often than Kevin and I had. We'd use Kevin's room. He could meet her in the bar, buy her dinner, and then take her up to his room. A very natural chain of events. Of course, I'd already be there waiting for them, having let myself in. Once the three of us were there, Kevin could call for room service, and Al Nuss could deliver the stuff. Once

204

the four of us were together, we could go over my plan.

Al's part was already clear. He was supplying transportation. Kevin, Christine, and I would put together what we saw while we were in the house, which should give us a pretty accurate picture of the layout around that locked room.

Any action taken toward getting the papers out of the house would be taken by Kevin and myself. The only thing I might use Christine for would be a diversion of some kind. If we couldn't work it out surreptitiously, then we'd have to work it like a holdup.

That idea appealed to me. Kevin and I could be a couple of holdup artists who worked our way into the house to rip it off. We'd have to handle the bodyguards, but that could be worked out. We could loot the house, taking whatever valuables Orantes had, plus the papers. As far as he was concerned, we'd be two guys who didn't know what we had.

I'd approach Kevin with the idea and get his thoughts on it. My original thinking had been to have one of us slip out of the room, ostensibly to go to the men's room, and then pick the lock and find the papers. Last night, however, we had discovered that the bathroom used for the men was in the other direction, down the hall, away from the steps. If we tried to slip up the stairs, we'd be sure to be seen by José. Christine could get upstairs, but she wouldn't know what to do once she got there, and I wouldn't put her in that position even if she did. I only wanted Kevin and myself leaving on that chopper. I wanted Christine to go back to the hotel, just another victim.

Back in my room I wondered how Christine was doing. I wondered how she felt when she looked out that window and saw the bloody, broken body of my assailant splattered on the ground, surrounded by shards of glass.

What was she telling the manager and his security man now?

Was she anything more than she appeared to be?

I'd find out soon enough. If she told them anything other than what we had agreed on, they'd be knocking at my door at any moment.

I called Kevin's room but got no answer. I tried again half an hour later, still no answer. A half hour after that the phone rang. It was Christine.

"How'd it go?" I asked.

"Fine . . . I guess. Nick, they said he didn't work for the hotel."

"I didn't think he did. It made your story easier to believe," I explained.

"Yes. They said I wasn't to worry about anything, and that I didn't even have to pay my hotel bill. They apologized to me, Nick. I couldn't believe it!"

"Chris, I want you to have dinner with Joseph James."

"Is he one of the other people you were talking about?"

"Yes. Call the desk and leave a message for him to call you. When he does, make the dinner date."

"Will he know why?"

"No, you tell him at dinner."

"What do I do afterward? He's a playboy and a charmer; he'll want me to go back to his room with him, no matter what the reason for dinner is."

"Then go."

Maybe I was testing her by not telling her that I'd be waiting in the room for the both of them.

She paused a moment, then said, "All right. If you say so."

"I'll see you later. You did fine Christine."

"Thanks."

It was time to contact Hawk.

I converted my TV again, and his face appeared on the screen.

"Well, N3, I've been wondering when I'd hear from you. As a matter of fact, I was wondering *if* I'd hear from you. Any sign of the Specialist?"

I told him about the second shooting incident.

"You're quite right. His behavior has been rather odd. How has the assignment been going?"

I told him that Casey had made contact, but had come away empty. I also told him that Casey and Trumball were working on another plan.

"And what about you?"

"Me? I'm just backup."

"I see."

Which meant he saw the way I wanted to play it. He was used to my going my own way on occasion. Sometimes he accepted it, and sometimes he didn't.

His decision not to ask further questions told me that this was a case of the former.

I asked him the question I had been wanting to ask.

"Sir, who requested me for this assignment?"

"I don't see where that's pertinent—"

"Was it Lamb? Colonel James J. Lamb, Casey's superior?" I asked.

"You seem to know the answer to that already," he told me.

"Yeah."

"What are you up to?" he asked.

"It's not what I'm up to," I told him. "It's where."

"All right, where?" he asked like a true straight man.

I held my palm flat, placing the side to my neck, and said, "To here."

CHAPTER THIRTY-FIVE

I let myself into Kevin's room about eight that evening. I settled myself onto the couch, with nothing to drink or read, and began going over the events that had occurred since my arrival on the island. I took them step by step and was still convinced that I was doing the right thing. I decided Casey and Trumball could never come up with a plan good enough for them to end up with the papers. I was flaunting protocol by going ahead without them, but I felt it was necessary. They were more of a liability than an asset.

I had actually started to doze off when I heard Kevin's key in the door. He was talking to Christine as they entered the room, turning on the charm, saying how nice it was for me to have arranged for them to have dinner together.

"My motives were not all that unselfish, Kevin," I told him.

They both stared at me in surprise, and a look of understanding crossed Christine's face. Kevin looked disappointed. He'd had visions of sugarplums dancing in his head, and I had dashed them to the ground.

"I see. This is our little meeting, eh, old man?"

"That's right, old man."

"Ah, well, I should have known it was too good to be true. I've never known you to share a woman willingly."

"Is that so?" Christine asked, amused. "You two are old friends, then?"

"We've gone round 'n' round once or twice before," Kevin said, exhibiting a gift for understatement.

"At least," I affirmed.

"Where's our fourth member?" Kevin asked.

"Order something from room service—he'll deliver," I told him.

Christine sat down on the couch, obviously relieved that the wrestling match with Kevin had been postponed.

"Wine for everyone?" he asked. We both nodded.

"Your choice," I told Kevin.

He called room service and ordered a bottle of wine. He was about to order four glasses, but I held up two fingers and he corrected himself in time.

When he hung up I said, "It's only supposed to be you and Christine, Kevin. When Al makes the delivery, he'll supply the extra glasses."

"Al who?" he asked.

"Kevin who?" Christine asked.

I explained to Kevin that the bellboy I had told him about was Al Nuss. Then I explained to Christine that Joe's real name was Kevin Joseph James Bagley.

"Impressive," she told him.

"That's what my parents thought," he told her.

"Are you really Nick Collins?" she asked me unexpectedly.

Before I could answer Kevin said, "Nick is ever and always, undeniably, Nick."

That seemed to satisfy her, and I thanked Kevin with a look.

At that point there was a knock on the door, and Al

Nuss announced, "Room service."

Kevin let him in, and he produced one bottle of red wine and four glasses.

I introduced each member of the team, and we all found seats: Christine and I on the couch, Al Nuss and Kevin on the other two chairs.

"Now what?" Kevin asked.

"Now we go over everything the three of us saw in Orantes's house last night. We'll put it together and come up with a pretty decent picture of the area of that house we're concerned with. I'll go first."

I told them what I saw when I went out of the room and down the hall to the john. I had seen a hallway, empty of furniture and a stairway—at least, ten of the twelve steps that led to the first landing—and the locked door. I had counted the steps when Orantes was showing us the house. There were another dozen up to the second floor.

What did I see? Not a whole lot. Then Kevin picked up where I left off.

"I saw the same thing," he told me. "There are no windows in the hall. There are also no windows in the men's room. There are no ducts in the ceiling. Nothing."

"Chris? What was upstairs?"

"The ladies' room was first door on the right," she said, looking up at the ceiling as if her memories were reflected there. "No ducts, no furniture in the upstairs hall. The bathroom itself was pretty bare, uh, no windows, only one door." She shrugged and said, "That's it."

I looked at the floor and said, "Nothing."

Silence ruled the room until Al Nuss broke it up.

"This looks like a wake," he announced. He grabbed the bottle and said, "Who wants more? C'mon, liven up. I don't know much about this caper, but there's got to be a way to get into this room you're talking about."

We all let him fill our glasses and then I said, "There is a way."

"How?" Christine asked, taking up the question.

"Orantes."

"The big man himself?" Nuss asked.

"Yeah. The way we get in is that he lets us in," I told them.

"Not willingly," Kevin remarked, shaking his head.

"No. At gunpoint."

Kevin made a face and said, "No finesse."

"You know what I have in mind?"

"I know how your mind works, Nicholas."

"Well, I don't," Christine said, "and I'm not sure I ever will."

"I think I do," Nuss said, "but fill the little lady in."

"We'll have to do it the sloppy way," I told her. "We'll go in to play poker. At a designated time during the game, Kevin or I will get up to get our own drink. It will be whichever of us has to cross in front of José—or whichever bodyguard it is that night—to do so. Once that one of us gets the drop on the bodyguard, the other will stand up and cover the rest of the players."

"Including me," Christine said.

"Including you," I agreed. "One of us will cover the room, the other will take Orantes upstairs and into his little locked room."

"What if he won't let you in?" she asked.

"At that point there are any number of ways to get in, with or without his cooperation," I explained.

"What happens if he calls the police?"

"Not him," Al Nuss. "He's likely to go after them himself, but he'd never call the cops. That's not his style."

"You'd have to get off the island before his men caught you," Christine said.

"That's where Al comes in," I said, nodding at Nuss.

"He'll have a copter waiting down at Orantes's dock for us. We'll disable the two boats that are tied up there, then take off in the chopper. You and the other players, Christine, will go back to the hotel, or wherever they want to go. You go to the hotel and take the morning shuttle off the island. Get out of here before Orantes starts to think about others being involved. In fact," I said, having a second thought, "maybe you shouldn't even come to the house. If this is the way we're going to do it, you would serve no constructive purpose by being there."

She shook her head firmly.

"Isn't there a chance that he would become suspicious, maybe wonder why all of a sudden it wasn't so important to me to play in his game?"

"That's possible, but you'll be off the island the next day, anyway," I argued.

"Why take a chance, Nick? I'll go in, and be held up, like everyone else. You will have to rob everyone else there, won't you? Just to make him believe that you really are robbers, and nothing more?"

"She's right, Nicholas. If she's not there to be robbed, he's going to wonder why, afterward. We don't have to worry about him looking for us later on. Why should she?"

They were both right, and I was forced to give in.

"My part in this seems so small," complained Al Nuss.

"Yours is the important part, Al," I told him. "You're going to get Kevin and myself off this island alive."

"Uh, I hate to bring this up, but where do we meet for the split?"

"I'll work that out with you later," I told him. "In any case, since there'll be some pretty wealthy people at that poker table, playing for some high stakes, why don't we just pass you whatever we get off of them, until we can meet and split the rest?"

He liked that idea.

"That sounds fair," he said.

"I thought it would," I said. A look at Kevin, however, said that he didn't think it was. He had also been thinking of all that money at the table.

Again I realized that I was going to have to think of some way to make this worth Kevin's while.

CHAPTER THIRTY-SIX

After the meeting, I walked Christine back to her room, Al Nuss took the room service tray back, and Kevin went downstairs to gamble and check out the female populace. I had no doubt that within the hour he'd be back in his room with a willing substitute for Christine.

"Coming in?" Christine asked.

"Uh, I don't think so."

She looked disappointed.

"I still have something to attend to," I explained.

"Something, or someone?" she asked.

"Now, now, let's not be catty. It's not becoming."

"And it's beneath me," she added.

"Right."

"But it's my right as a woman," she reminded me. She gave me a long kiss, as if to tell me that this was what I was missing. The reminder was nice, but I really didn't need it. I knew what I'd be missing.

"See you tomorrow," I told her when I got my breath back.

"If not sooner," she whispered, and slipped into her room. I left before I could give in to the urge to knock on her door.

In my room I found what I thought I'd find.

Casey.

She'd let herself into my room the same way I let myself into Kevin's.

She was draped prettily across my couch, wearing a flowing white nightgown. There was a bottle of champagne and two glasses on the coffee table.

There had been something we hadn't discussed at our little meeting, like what we would do about Casey when the time came for our big holdup.

Or what Casey would do.

I hadn't brought it up because I expected Casey to be waiting for me in my room. I intended to take care of that detail myself.

"Well, what a surprise," I said.

"I'll bet," she replied. She had her elbow on the back of the couch and her head in her right hand, with the index finger along her temple and her pinky along her chin. The rest of her fingers were bunched against her cheek. It was a classic pose, and she executed it quite well.

"Come and sit," she invited.

I did as she said. I sat, popped the cork on the chilled champagne, and poured two glasses. When I handed hers to her she took it left-handed, retaining her pose with the right hand.

"Cheers," I said, and we clinked glasses and drank.

"You're up to something," she told me.

"Am I?" I asked innocently.

"Of course. You couldn't be Nick Carter and not be up to something," she explained.

"I see," I said. Leaning close to her and putting my mouth less than an inch from hers, I said, "And you're here to seduce it out of me, right?"

I wasn't sure what her reaction would be. She was

capable of flying into a rage, pulling rank, and demanding an explanation, or she could little-girl it.

When she went into her pout, I knew she was going to try and little-girl it—which meant that when that didn't work, her rage would be even worse.

"How could you think that of me?" she asked.

"I know you, Casey," I told her, getting up from the couch and taking off my jacket.

She dropped her right hand, reached over, and put her glass down on the coffee table.

"I don't think you do, Nick," she told me. "I don't think you do, at all."

She surprised me. She'd dropped the little-girl act, but she hadn't gone the other way, as I had expected.

She'd gone middle-of-the-road on me.

"I want to get this job done, Nick. My first plan didn't work quite up to my expectations. I'll admit that much. Allan and I haven't come up with anything much better. If you've got an idea, let me hear it."

This was quite a change of pace.

Something started to bother me then, but I tabled it for another time.

"All right, I do have an idea," I admitted.

"What is it?" she asked quickly.

"Well, I'm not ready to share it, not just yet," I told her.

"Are you worried about Allan?"

"That's part of it. If I tell you, you'll have to tell him."

"He's my partner," she reasoned.

"I know that. Look," I said, sitting next to her again, "we'll be out at Orantes's house again tomorrow night. Just follow my lead. Whatever I do, play along. If you want to get this job done, you'll trust me."

It went against the grain. She was in charge and I was backup. I was supposed to follow her lead, not vice versa.

"All right," she said.

"What will you tell Allan?"

"What can I tell him? You haven't told me anything. We'll play it the same way. I'll carry a mike, and he'll monitor me from the hotel room."

"And you'll follow my lead?"

She reclaimed her previous pose and said, "Lead on."

I did, to the bedroom, and she followed along very nicely indeed.

Going to bed with Casey was very pleasant, but neither one of us was all there. We went through the motions well enough, but both of us had other things on our minds.

Afterward, she didn't stay the night but got dressed and went back to her room. I had no doubt that she'd replay our entire conversation to Trumball. After all, they were partners.

I felt better about Christine's part in all of this. It was nil. She'd be getting held up, like the rest of the players, and that would be that. No one could suspect her for that. I did wish that I could have kept her out of it altogether, but this was the next best thing.

I intended to meet with Al Nuss in the morning and arrange to meet him for "the split," probably in Washington, when it was all over. I'd explain it all to him then. Maybe I could get him to be satisfied with what we got from the players. After all, it would be quite a substantial sum, the stakes of the game being what they were.

Kevin was another story. He'd have to come out of this with a hell of a lot to satisfy him, because he was going against the people who hired him to bid, plus he was going against Orantes. I was going to have to make it worth his while. The prospect of facing an irate Kevin Bagley was not at all pleasant.

I was pretty sure, however, that I could make it worth

his while, but that remained to be seen.

I was playing a dangerous game, juggling everybody's welfare, or maybe even their lives. I was juggling Al Nuss, Christine Hall, and Kevin Bagley, who were all helping me for different reasons, none of which had anything to do with what was really going on. I was juggling Casey and Trumball, trying to keep them in the dark about my plan, for which I felt more than justified. After all, they'd been keeping me in the dark for as long as I'd been on the island. I felt no guilt about deceiving them.

I didn't feel much guilt about deceiving Nuss and Kevin, either. Nuss was a schemer and Kevin was a mercenary. I was just hoping I could handle them afterward, when they found out that I might not be able to deliver all that I'd promised.

Christine I felt guilty about. I had come to believe that she was nothing more than what she seemed, and I felt badly about playing on her desire for some excitement.

That wouldn't stop me from using her, though. That was what this business was all about.

CHAPTER THIRTY-SEVEN

The next morning I ordered breakfast and as planned it was Al Nuss who delivered it.

He gave me a chance to sit, but before I could butter my muffin he said, "So?" getting right to the point.

"So, what?"

"Where do we make the split?"

"You want half my muffin?" I offered.

"Okay, okay, I'm sorry. Eat your breakfast."

"No, Al, it's okay," I told him. I buttered my muffin and told him to sit and have a cup of coffee.

"We'll go tonight, Al. Are you sure you can get the chopper?"

"No problem. He's standing by. Where do you want him to take you?"

"To the nearest place where we can get a commercial flight," I told him. "You and I will meet in Washington, three days from today." I gave him the name of a hotel and the number of the room that would be reserved for him.

"You'll be there?" he asked.

"Yeah, I'll be there, Al, but the money from the game is yours, like I said last night."

"Your friend didn't like that part," he pointed out. He was talking about Kevin.

"You noticed that, huh? Don't worry about Kevin. I'll handle him."

"You know something, Nick?" he said, rising and taking the breakfast cart to the door. I had my coffee and muffin on the end table.

"What?"

He opened the door, but before he went out he said, "I get the feeling that you're handling all of us."

And he left.

He was right, of course. I only hoped that I was doing it well.

I called Kevin and arranged to meet him for lunch. I called Christine and told her I was sorry I hadn't stopped by her room last night.

"Was I expecting you?" she asked.

"I thought you might have been."

"Well, I might have been," she conceded. "How did that 'something' you had to attend to go?"

"It went okay. It had to do with tonight."

"Oh, yeah, tonight," she said flatly.

"Christine, you can still change your mind, you know."

"No, no, I don't want to do that," she assured me.

"You don't sound so sure."

"Nick," she scolded. "I'm sure."

"Okay, okay."

"How about lunch?"

"I have to see, uh, someone for lunch."

"Someone?"

"One of our friends," I said.

"Oh. About tonight?"

"Yes."

"Can we have dinner?"

"I don't see why not."

"And talk?"

"About tonight?"

"I just need a little reassuring," she told me. "That doesn't mean I'm changing my mind."

I smiled and just barely kept from laughing.

"I'll pick you up at your room at seven," I told her.

"Great. See you then."

Orantes's car would arrive at nine o'clock again. I thought it advisable that we either travel in separate cars or else share one with one or more of the other players. I did not want just the two of us to share a car. I didn't want any undue attention placed on the both of us together.

I met Kevin on the veranda for lunch, which turned out to be the liquid variety.

"Have you got a gun?" I asked.

"Nicholas, I came to bid, not to rob," he reminded me.

Kevin was very good with a gun, but he didn't carry one unless he had to.

"Okay, Al Nuss can get you one."

"A Beretta would be nice," he told me.

"Nine millimeter?"

"Short?"

"Right."

"We go one hour after we start the game," I told him. "Whichever one of us is closest to the bodyguard will take him out."

"Take him out?"

"Yeah, there's no point in having him awake. He might decide to be a hero. We should be able to handle the others."

"Orantes?"

"I don't think he does his own killing, Kevin. If he doesn't have someone around to order it done, I don't think he'll try it."

"You won't mind if I keep one eye on him and the other on everyone else anyway, will you?"

"No. It doesn't hurt to be careful. I'll take him off your hands, though."

"I see. I'll hold everyone downstairs, and you take the big man upstairs and get the papers."

"And anything else that's not nailed down."

"You wouldn't pop off and leave me holding the bag, would you, old boy?" he asked.

"Kevin, have I ever?"

"That time in Honolulu—"

"Never mind. I give you my word, we'll leave that house together."

"Well, I suppose that will have to do, won't it?"

"It's all I've got."

In between lunch with Kevin and dinner with Christine, I took delivery from Al Nuss on Kevin's gun.

"Did you get the Beretta?" I asked.

"Close," he told me, handing me the package. We were in his room. I opened up the package and removed a six-shot, .32 Colt Police Positive.

I looked at him.

"Close?"

He shrugged. "That was as close as I could get."

"It'll do—if it works."

"It works," he assured me.

At dinner with Christine, I went over with her just the way it would work.

"You're going to kill the bodyguard?" she asked, misunderstanding me when I told her that one of us would "take out" the bodyguard.

"No, we'll just put him to sleep so he doesn't get brave."

"Nick?"

"Yeah?"

"What are you going to do with the bride?"
I scratched my head.
"I think I'll leave her to Kevin."

CHAPTER THIRTY-EIGHT

We were fifty minutes into the game—ten minutes from our deadline—when things started to look like they'd go wrong.

José was bodyguard again, holding the same pose that he had held the other night. Kevin was closest to him, so he was going to be the one to take him out.

So with ten minutes to go, José's twin brother walked in—in the person of one of Orantes's army of interchangeable bodyguards. He entered the room and took up position at the door.

Now, Kevin could still take out José, but this second guy wouldn't just stand there and watch. I was going to have to handle bodyguard number two and just hope that we wouldn't end up trading shots. Not only would someone end up getting hurt—like Christine or even Casey—but it would alert the rest of Orantes's men, either in the house or on the grounds, and we weren't at all sure just how many of them there were.

We had to do this with a minimum of noise.

With five minutes to go, Kevin was beginning to sweat it. He looked at me, and I tried to give him the go-ahead with my eyes and hoped he caught it. He had to trust me enough to go ahead with the plan.

He did.

Exactly one hour after we started the game, he stretched and said, "I need one of my special drinks."

"Tell Casey," Orantes told him.

"No, no, this is a family brew," he told Orantes, rising from his seat. "I'll make it myself."

"José!"

I moved as soon as I heard Orantes's voice.

Wilhelmina was in my hand and pointing at the body-guard on the door. His hand stopped halfway to his belt. I didn't have to look to know that José was pointing a gun at Kevin, who had frozen in his tracks right by his chair.

"This looks like a stand-off, Mr. Collins," Orantes announced. "You shoot my man, and José shoots yours. Then we get to see which one of you is the faster. I'll bet on José."

"You'd lose," Casey said from the bar. I couldn't afford to turn my head and look at her, but I didn't have to. She let us all know what was going on.

"I've got a gun pointed at your big, fat head, Oswaldo, baby," she said, "and if I hear a shot I'm going to blow it right off your fat shoulders."

I chanced a glance at Kevin, who was looking beyond Orantes at Casey. The look on his face told me that she wasn't running a bluff.

There was a long period of silence while Orantes decided what to do. Finally I heard him say, "José."

When Kevin moved, I knew José had lowered his gun. I motioned to the other bodyguard to remove his from his hip and drop it to the floor.

I got up from my seat and told him to sit in it. Kevin did the same with José.

"Okay, now everybody put their hands on the table," I instructed.

"What the hell—" Tex began, but I cut him off.

"We don't want or need any arguments," I warned everyone in general. "I want all hands on the tabletop—now!"

They did as they were instructed, including Christine, who was looking properly frightened, and probably was.

Casey came around from behind the bar and covered the table with her gun.

"Nice job of following my lead," I told her, only now we had another passenger for the helicopter. I couldn't leave her behind now that she'd revealed herself.

Who had given us away to Orantes, though? He had been ready for Kevin's move, and had brought in some backup firepower. We were lucky to have gotten away with the takeover without a shot being fired.

Thanks to Casey.

"Kevin, you and Casey take care of everyone here," I told him.

"Right." He had his gun out, and José's was in his belt. I picked up the other bodyguard's discarded gun and stuffed it in my belt.

"Okay, fat man," I said, sounding like an old movie, "up."

When he didn't move, Casey prodded the back of his head with her gun. "The man said *up*," she reminded him.

He got up reluctantly, with his hands in view. His palms were sweaty, and his forehead was beading up.

The big man had lost his poker face.

"Let's go upstairs," I told him.

"There's nothing up there of any value, I assure you," he told me.

"No? There's a locked door up there, one that you ignored when you gave us the tour the other night. I want to see what's behind it."

"I assure you—"

"Why don't we just send him to meet his maker, old

boy," Kevin suggested, "and break the lock?"

Orantes didn't like that suggestion.

"No, I'm sure Mr. Orantes would much rather use his key and open the door for me, wouldn't you?"

Orantes looked resigned, and got out from behind the table.

"Easy," I told him. "Hands in view at all times. Let's go."

I let him precede me out of the room, and behind me I heard Kevin go into his spiel.

"Ladies and gentlemen, it's contribution time . . ."

As we started ascending the stairs Orantes said, "Carter, we can work out a deal."

The fact that he'd used my real name almost got by me.

"What kind of a deal?"

"Money, plenty of it. Millions, if you like."

Right then I was glad I was the one taking him upstairs and not Kevin. My English friend might have found that an offer too good to refuse.

"I think I'll pass, pal."

"You're mad."

"Not yet, but keep talking like that and you're likely to get me pissed."

When we reached the door I said, "Key, left hand, and carefully."

He plucked it out, then did a half-turn toward me.

"Look, Carter—"

"No deals," I told him. "Open it."

He fit the key into the lock with the greatest of reluctance, and then swung the door inward. I pushed him in ahead of me and followed.

It was a small, compact room, and I could see why he kept it locked. The room was filled with objects d'art, from paintings on the walls to sculptures on various tables, and a desk.

I shut the door behind me.

"Since you know who I really am, Orantes, you know what I'm here for. Where is it?"

"I'm sure I don't know—"

"This room looks soundproof," I said, checking the walls and ceilings with my eyes.

"It is."

"That's good, because in two minutes I'm going to start using some of these valuable sculptures of yours for target practice."

"You can't—"

"Then I'll start shooting the eyes out of some of these portraits."

"Carter, look, our deal—"

I took his bodyguard's .45 from my belt and blew a piece of sculpture off his desk.

"No! That was a priceless—"

"Now it's in pieces. Where are the notes?"

He stared at the pieces on the floor and his resolve broke.

"In the safe."

"Open it."

He walked behind his desk, careful not to step on the pieces of clay on the floor. He swung a hinged painting away from the wall and revealed a small safe. I stuffed the .45 back into my belt and switched Wilhelmina to my right hand. I gave him plenty of rope, and he went and hung himself.

He stuck his hand into the safe, and I allowed him to get the gun out and turn halfway before I shot him. I did that because he now knew that this was not just a hold-up, and I didn't want word to get out that the notes had been taken by the United States government.

He fell to the floor, right on top of the pieces of his priceless sculpture. Now neither one of them was worth anything.

I stepped over him—no easy task in itself—and rifled through the safe. I came up with various articles of men's jewelry and a manila packet. I opened the packet and found what I wanted inside. I closed it up again and tucked it away in my inside jacket pocket.

As an afterthought, I tucked some of the more expensive pieces of jewelry into my pockets for Al Nuss—just to keep him happy.

I kept Wilhelmina handy as I crossed the room and opened the door to leave. I didn't really anticipate any further trouble, but that just shows you how wrong a guy can be.

As I closed the door behind me, I heard a scream and then, in rapid succession, four shots from two different guns.

CHAPTER THIRTY-NINE

As I ran down the stairs I saw the people who had been seated around the table run out of the poker room and down the hall. I didn't see Kevin, Christine, or Casey. Nor did I see the two bodyguards.

When I entered the room it looked like a battlefield. One of the bodyguards was sprawled out on the poker table, his blood soaking the green felt a deep red. The other—José—was on the floor with a good portion of his head blown away.

There was a third body, too.

Kevin Bagley would smile and charm no more. He was lying by the bar with two holes in his chest and a surprised look on his face.

The only other two people in the room were Christine and myself.

Casey was gone.

I hadn't seen her run from the room, but she could have gotten out ahead of the rest of the people.

"Christine, what happened?"

She looked dazed, standing against one wall, where she must have flattened herself when the shooting started.

"I'm not sure," she told me. "It happened so fast. One

of them got a gun from somewhere," she said, indicating the two bodyguards.

She pointed to José.

"Then the shooting started—"

"Who fired first?"

She shrugged helplessly, at a loss for words.

"Where's Casey?"

Again, she opened her mouth but nothing much came out.

I didn't have time to try and drag it out of her. The grounds would soon be alive with Orantes's men, looking for him and stopping anyone they didn't know.

I grabbed her hand and said, "C'mon, let's get down to the dock. We'll have to take that chopper."

I half dragged her down the hall and out the front door. Some of the players from the game were wandering about aimlessly, looking for a car or something to get them off the grounds. J.W. Farrel was standing at the bottom of the steps, wringing his hands and wailing. Tex was telling him to "Shaddup!"

"Nick!" Chris shouted.

"C'mon," I told her, pulling her down the front steps.

"Nick, I have to tell you—"

"Later."

Coming up the road from the direction of the front gate were two of Orantes's men. Both were armed with pump action shotguns, and they were obviously not shy about using them on anyone they didn't recognize.

One of them blew J.W. Farrel halfway up the steps, and the other fixed Jock "Tex" Owens so he wouldn't ever have to worry about combing his hair again.

"Oh, my God!" Christine shouted.

I brought Wilhelmina up and fired twice at the two armed men. One of them yelled and went down; the other had been moving when I fired and escaped injury. He brought his shotgun around and fired in our direction. I pushed Christine away and dove after her. A couple of stray pellets found their way into the thigh of my injured leg, but the brunt of the blast went by harmlessly.

"Let's move," I advised Christine. "This way."

I grabbed her and we started for the side gate, which would lead outside the grounds to the stairs down the cliff, then to the dock, and, hopefully, to the chopper.

There was a lot of shouting behind us and the occasional report of a shotgun. All of Orantes's men must have been armed with them. They must have been blowing hell out of what was left of the poker players, and frantically looking for their boss.

"Wait," I told her. I spotted a path in the brush, which would hopefully lead to the side gate. "This way."

We plunged down the path and I kept alert for anyone following us, or anyone who might have been ahead.

Where was Casey, and was she alive or dead?

The path we were on did lead directly to the side gate —and to the guard who was standing in front of it. As we approached he raised his shotgun, and I let three quick shots go from Wilhelmina. I couldn't stop him from pulling the trigger, but his shot was into the sky as he twisted and fell to the ground, dead. We stepped over him to the gate and found it locked.

"Damn," I shouted. I didn't waste time. I grabbed the dead guard's shotgun, pointed it at the lock, and let a shot go. The lock scattered and the gate swung open.

I grabbed her hand and dragged her out and across the road to the head of the steps.

"They're steep," I told her, "but we've got to move as quickly as we can."

"I understand."

I wasn't sure whether to let her go first, or to go ahead of her. If I went first, I could catch her if she fell, but if some of Orantes's men made it to the top of the steps before we made it to the bottom, she'd be in the line of fire. I decided to go for speed, and we could go faster with me in the lead.

"Get rid of your shoes," I told her. I didn't want her tripping on her heels. She kicked them off and we started down.

I could see the chopper at the dock, and obviously he saw us because he kicked his engine into life and the rotor began to turn.

Christine slipped once, but I was able to keep her from tumbling down the remaining steps. We reached the bottom without any gunfire from the top, so we were practically home free.

Or so I thought.

As we approached the helicopter, someone got out of it. I couldn't see who it was because of the way he was dressed. All dark clothing, with a dark hood over his head. I assumed it was a man, because the figure was tall and slim. He stood with his hands on his hips and his feet planted apart.

I knew who he was.

"Oh, great," I said.

"What?" Christine asked.

"It's time," I said. "It's a lousy time, but it's time."

My whole leg was throbbing as a result of the run from the house and the trip down the steep steps to the dock.

"Back away, Christine," I warned her.

The Specialist had finally made his move.

He started to advance on me, and there were no weapons in his hands. He had decided to take me on hand to hand, but he had made one mistake.

I didn't have the time. Much as I would have liked to test him—and myself—I just couldn't afford to stop right now.

I raised Wilhelmina and pulled her trigger twice.

The result was two empty clicks. In the excitement, I had not been counting my shots. I was out of ammunition. And the .45 in my belt had fallen out just as we reached the bottom of the staircase. Now I was forced to test myself against the number-one assassin in the world over the last four years.

I put Wilhelmina back in place under my arm, and moved toward the Specialist.

He was quick, there was no denying that. He moved in fast, but I avoided him by pivoting away—on my bad foot. The pain went from my ankle to my calf and up through my thigh, and it was exquisite. I went down on one knee, and my opponent was quick to seize his opportunity. As he came in on me I saw the glint of the knife in his hand. He'd thrown me off by showing me his empty hands, but he'd had a knife tucked away and he was about to disembowel me. I dove in beneath his charge, flicked Hugo into my hand, and drove him hilt-deep into the Specialist's belly. He hadn't expected that at all.

His scream echoed in my ears, then died with him. I lowered him off my shoulder to the dock, and then removed his hood. I couldn't believe what I saw and let out a low groan.

"What is it?" Christine asked. "Are you all right?"

"There's something wrong here," I told her.

"Wha—"

I stood up, shaking my head, and stared down at the face of Allan Trumball—the Specialist?

There was no way I could buy Allan Trumball as the Specialist, the deadliest, most accurate killer in the world: I had killed him too easily.

"Nick?" Christine said.

"What?"

I turned to look at her, but she was pointing beyond me to the end of the dock.

I looked around in time to see a second figure—identically clad in dark clothing and a hood—step from the helicopter.

"What's this," I muttered.

I looked behind us, but there was no one coming down the cliff steps after us—yet.

"Another one?" she asked.

"I think this one is *the* one," I told her. "The first team."

The new figure stood just outside the helicopter, watching us. This one was not as tall as the first, nor did he figure on playing the scene the same way the first one did. He was holding a Beretta in one hand, but pointed down at the dock.

"Nick!"

"Stay behind me, Christine. If that gun comes up, I'm going to have to dive for the forty-five at the bottom of the staircase."

I felt silly. I felt like an Old West gunfighter waiting for the other guy to go for his gun.

It was so quiet I could hear the water lapping up against the sides of the two boats and the two boats bumping up against the dock.

C'mon, c'mon, I was thinking, go for your gun.

But it was the other hand that came up, the one without the gun. It was a movement that was meant to freeze me in my tracks. The surprise was supposed to make me hesitate long enough to be shot full of holes, but as that hand went up, up, up and grasped the top of the hood, pulling it off to reveal the identity of the person beneath, I went for the .45 and blew Casey Laurence right off the dock.

CHAPTER FORTY

"And after that?" Hawk asked.

We were in his office two days after the dock incident. I was filling him in on the whole Pleasure Island thing, and leading up to the punchline.

"After that we found the pilot floating right alongside her."

"You flew the helicopter?" he asked.

"No. As a matter of fact Christine did. It was something else she once tried for, you know, excitement. It came in pretty handy, too."

Christine Hall had indeed been nothing more than what she seemed: a lady gambler in search of some momentary excitement in her life—and a helicopter pilot to boot.

"The explosives we needed were in the helicopter," I went on. "And we disabled the two boats just in case any more of Orantes's men were around and decided to give us a chase."

"Disabled?"

"We sunk them."

"And the notes?"

"Oh, yeah, the notes," I said, touching my breast pocket. "Were they really what it was all about?" I

asked, taking the packet out and placing it on my side of
his desk.

"What else would it be about?" he asked.

"Why don't we ask Colonel James J. Lamb?" I suggested.

"Why Lamb?"

"Can we do this without playing games?" I asked, getting annoyed. "I was kept in the dark from day one on
this thing, starting with you. I think I was put on Pleasure Island as bait. What I want to know is, who put me
on the hook?"

He drummed his fingertips on his desk a few times,
the only outward indication that he was giving my question any serious consideration.

"I guess I did," he finally said.

"You?" I had convinced myself that when I found out
for sure who it was, it wouldn't be Hawk.

"Would you care to explain that?"

"N3—" he began in that stern I'm-the-boss-and-I-
don't-have-to-explain-everything-to-you tone of voice.

"Look, if you hung me out on a line to dry, I think I
deserve to know why," I told him.

I think he realized he couldn't shake me off on this.
The muscles in his jaw rippled just before he started to
speak.

"For some time now—over a year, in fact—I've had
my suspicions about Lamb," he began. "I thought he
was using his position as head of a branch of the American Secret Service to run his own operation on the side."

"What kind of an operation?"

"A murder squad."

I started to understand.

"Research revealed a series of coincidences, and the
magic number in every case was four." He ticked them
off on his fingers as he explained. "Lamb was put in

charge of his branch of the service four years ago. Two: The Specialist made his first appearance four years ago. Three: Among a number of new agents inducted into the service four years ago—Lamb's branch of the service—were Allan Trumball and Casey Laurence."

"They weren't the only ones," I told him.

"No, they weren't." He looked at the ceiling, refreshing his memory. "There were forty-three new agents inducted, and six of them went to Lamb. I had checked out the other four prior to the Pleasure Island affair, and was convinced that they were not involved."

"That left Casey and Trumball."

"I was going to assign you, N3, to shadow them until you were satisfied one way or the other, but Lamb made it easier for me. He asked if he could borrow you for the Pleasure Island assignment, and I agreed."

"I see. You surmised that I was the next victim."

He nodded.

"There could be no other reason for Lamb to request you. Nick Carter was not your everyday backup agent. You almost put a crimp in my plans by getting hurt on your last assignment, but that made it easier for me to agree with Lamb without seeming like I was giving in too easily. I told him I was glad to have something relatively easy to put you on, just to keep you in circulation."

"So it's been Lamb who's been the brains behind the Specialist for the past four years. He took two agents, Casey and Trumball, combined their talents, and came up with one master assassin."

Again, he nodded. "He hired them out to anyone with enough money to pay. Of their first twenty-four victims, eight were American agents, the rest foreign agents of one government or another. You were to be their twenty-fifth victim."

"But who hired them?"

He shrugged. "That really isn't of any importance. It could have been any one of a dozen opposition agencies that you have dealt with in the past. I'm sure they're not the only ones who want to see you dead."

"I'm sure," I agreed. "And what about these?" I asked, picking up the packet of notes.

"Those are genuine," he told me, taking them from my hand.

"Well, for experienced agents, Casey and Trumball sure came up with a pretty poor plan to get them."

"That's because they weren't experienced agents. In the four years that they have 'worked' for Lamb, he never sent them on agency matters. All they did was kill."

"So they couldn't even put up a good front for my benefit. They didn't know how."

"Their only goal was to kill you."

I shook my head.

"I still can't see Trumball as even half of the Specialist."

"Obviously, he was guided by Miss Laurence, who was in turn guided by the colonel."

"All she had to do was point him in the right direction," I said, remembering a conversation I'd had with her.

"I still can't understand those deliberate misses," I told him, referring to the two shooting incidents. "That wasn't their style."

"There's no one to ask," Hawk pointed out. "You'll have to figure that one out for yourself."

Had it been Casey or Trumball? Or both—one the first time, and the other the second? Why would Trumball miss on purpose? He hated me. Were Casey's feelings about me that strong that she'd try to warn me? Was that what the warning on the roof had been about, too, when she told me she was afraid Trumball was going to try for me?

She'd been an agent, and a killer, but she was still a woman, and I had really given up trying to figure women out years ago.

"So the Specialist was really two people," I summed up, "or three, if you count Lamb."

"We hope," Hawk added. "It still remains to be seen."

"Are you going to leave Lamb in operation?" I asked.

"I don't really have any proof against him," he explained. "I might be able to get him removed from his office, but we'll have to see whether or not he recruits some new personnel and starts all over again."

"It might be easier to keep an eye on him if he stays in office," I pointed out.

"True. At least, as a result of all this, I am now one hundred percent sure that he is behind the Specialist. And thanks to you, the Specialist is out of business for a while."

"I wish there had been an easier way to do it, though," I told him.

"If there had been an easier way, N3," he told me, "I wouldn't have needed you."

True, I thought. He never did give me the easy ones.

"You should be grateful that I decided to supply you with some adequate backup."

"Backup?" I asked. "Kevin Bagley?"

"No, not Bagley. That was a coincidence."

An unfortunate one for Kevin, and I was sorry. I had genuinely liked him.

In the helicopter, Christine had told me what had happened in the cardroom. José had produced a .45 from somewhere—possibly a cache underneath the table —and it was he who shot Kevin twice in the chest. Casey then shot José and the second bodyguard once. After that all hell broke loose.

It was Christine who I heard scream, she admitted sheepishly.

"The man you knew as Al Nuss," he revealed, "was established at Pleasure Island as a bellboy to be there in the event you needed him."

"Al Nuss?" I asked. "I thought he was just a small-timer running a racket. He's on the payroll?"

"Not exactly. He's a freelance, and he was paid handsomely for what he did."

"I guess I won't be meeting him as planned, then," I said.

"Certainly not."

Which was kind of a relief. I had been trying to come up with a suitable explanation for meeting him empty-handed. I remembered Nuss always managing to be around, and now I knew why.

Probably the one thing I was the happiest about was Christine. She was apparently just what she seemed—I hoped.

"Was he the only one you sent in?"

"Yes."

"You're sure you didn't send Christine Hall in, too?"

"No, it went against my grain to even send you one backup; I wasn't about to send you two. I only sent you Nuss because of the injury to your foot."

All sentiment, Hawk, that's you—you good old buzzard!

"No," he continued, "Mrs. Hall was your own personal recruit, I'm afraid. I hope you won't be wanting us to supply you with some sort of payment for her," he said.

"No, sir," I told him, rising. My foot still bothered me some. I had twisted it pretty badly in the scuffle with Allan Trumball on the dock. I fully expected to have sufficient time off for it to heal. "No, I'll be supplying payment for Mrs. Hall in my own manner," I assured him.

In fact, she was in a hotel—the Washington hotel, as a matter of fact—waiting for me to pick her up for dinner. And after dinner, proper payment for all of her help.

"Well, N3, take a few days for your foot to heal properly," he said magnanimously. "I have something waiting on a back burner for you."

A few days?

"You're all heart, sir," I told him, hobbling to the door with the aid of my cane. My thigh was sore where those stray pellets had struck me.

He looked a little ill at the very prospect of what I had just said and replied, "I certainly hope not, N3."

FROM THE

NICK CARTER
KILLMASTER SERIES

☐ **TEMPLE OF FEAR**	80215-X	$1.75
☐ **THE NICHOVEV PLOT**	57435-1	$1.75
☐ **TIME CLOCK OF DEATH**	81025-X	$1.75
☐ **UNDER THE WALL**	84499-6	$1.75
☐ **THE PEMEX CHART**	65858-X	$1.95
☐ **SIGN OF THE PRAYER SHAWL**	76355-3	$1.75
☐ **THUNDERSTRUCK IN SYRIA**	80860-3	$1.95
☐ **THE MAN WHO SOLD DEATH**	51921-0	$1.75
☒ **THE SUICIDE SEAT**	79077-1	$2.25
☐ **SAFARI OF SPIES**	75330-2	$1.95
☐ **TURKISH BLOODBATH**	82726-8	$2.25
☐ **WAR FROM THE CLOUDS**	87192-5	$2.25
☐ **THE JUDAS SPY**	41295-5	$1.75

ⓒ ACE CHARTER BOOKS
P.O. Box 400, Kirkwood, N.Y. 13795   N-01

Please send me the titles checked above. I enclose _____.
Include 75¢ for postage and handling if one book is ordered; 50¢ per
book for two to five. If six or more are ordered, postage is free. California, Illinois, New York and Tennessee residents please add sales tax.

NAME_____

ADDRESS_____

CITY_____STATE_____ZIP_____

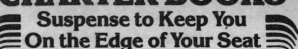